WISDOM OF THE WITCH

A WITCHES OF KEATING HOLLOW NOVELLA

KEATING HOLLOW HAPPILY EVER AFTERS
BOOK TWO

DEANNA CHASE

Copyright © 2024 by Deanna Chase

Editing: Angie Ramey

Cover image: © Ravven

ISBN 978-1-953422-94-1

All rights reserved. No part of this publication may be reproduced, stored in, or introduced into a retrieval system, or transmitted in any form, or by any means (electronic, mechanical, photocopying, recording, or otherwise) without the prior written permission of both the copyright owner and the publisher of this book.

This book is a work of fiction. Names, characters, places, and incidents are products of the author's imagination or are used fictitiously. Any resemblance to actual events, locals, business establishments, or persons, living or dead, are entirely coincidental.

Bayou Moon Press, LLC

www.deannachase.com

Printed in the United States of America

ABOUT THIS BOOK

Noel Townsend loves the life she's built for herself with her husband Drew and her two daughters. After years of running the Keating Hollow inn, Noel finally has hired help and has more time to devote to her new farm and her family. But when her youngest daughter encounters a spirit in their farmhouse, Noel suddenly finds herself in a fight for her life. It's going to take everything she has to get out of this one, along with the love and determination of her devoted husband, Drew Baker.

CHAPTER 1

"Okay, what kind of cookies are we making?" Noel Townsend-Baker asked her six-year-old as she opened the pantry door.

"Chocolate chip! No, wait... peanut butter!" Poppy called out as she chased Buffy, the brindle-colored shih tzu, around the kitchen island.

"Really? Peanut butter?" Noel asked her with a frown. Chocolate chip were her youngest daughter's favorite, and Noel couldn't remember a single time in the past year that Poppy hadn't requested them.

"Daddy likes peanut butter," Poppy said and gripped Buffy around the middle, hugging her to her chest. The little dog licked her face once and then wiggled out of her grip and ran into the living room.

"That's very sweet of you, baby," Noel said, grabbing

Poppy around the waist and giving her cheek a smacking kiss.

Poppy giggled and squirmed until she was free of her mother's embrace.

The front door opened and her other daughter, Daisy, called out, "I'm home."

"We're in here," Noel called out.

A moment later she heard her thirteen-year-old speaking to Buffy in a baby voice. "There's my pretty girl," Daisy said. "Did you miss me?"

Poppy darted into the living room to greet her sister, and Noel's heart filled with joy. It was Friday afternoon, she had the weekend off from work, and her girls were home, safe and happy. The only one missing was her husband, Drew, who was due home any minute now.

There was a loud knock on the door, followed by Buffy's incessant barking.

"Buffy, hush!" Daisy called out.

The front door opened, and familiar laughter filled the house.

Noel wiped her hands on a dish towel and went to find out what the commotion was all about. Her sister Abby was kneeling down, hugging Poppy, while her stepdaughter, Olive, was busy unleashing her golden retriever, Endora.

"Well, hello there," Noel said as Endora ran over,

demanding attention. Noel petted the dog's head and added, "I wasn't expecting you two until later." Daisy and Olive were having a sleepover, and Abby was planning to drop Olive off right before dinner.

Abby glanced up. "Sorry. I should've called. Olive's piano lesson was canceled. Uncle Chad's a little under the weather today."

"That's too bad. I'll give Hope a call later and see if they need anything," Noel said, referring to their youngest sister. "But I'm happy you two are here early. Can you stay for a bit? Poppy and I were just getting ready to make cookies."

"That's what I was planning." Abby looked at Poppy, who was still leaning into her. "What kind?"

"Peanut butter!" Poppy grabbed Abby by the hand and started tugging her aunt into the other room.

Noel laughed as she watched her daughter haul Abby into the kitchen.

Olive and Daisy had their heads together and were already planning their evening. The two cousins were good friends who hadn't seen each other in a while due to their busy schedules.

"Olive, come over here and give me a hug before you two disappear into Daisy's room."

Her niece ran over and wrapped her arms around Noel, squeezing her tight. "Your house looks wonderful, Aunt Noel. The last time I saw it the walls weren't even up yet."

Noel laughed. "Yeah, it looks a little different now." After Noel and Drew were married, they'd moved into his small, three-bedroom home. They'd finally sold it and purchased a fixer-upper on two acres just down the road from her father's house after Drew was promoted to town sheriff. After months of a major remodel, they'd finally moved in. "Want a tour?"

"Heck yes!" Olive glanced back and said, "Daisy, can you keep an eye on Endora? I don't want her messing anything up."

"Sure," Daisy said. "Check out the fancy dog bath in the mudroom. Endora's gonna love it."

"Fancy dog bath?" Olive asked Noel. "What's that? A dog spa?"

Noel laughed. "Sort of. Let me show you."

They walked into the kitchen, where they found Abby and Poppy searching one of the cupboards for something.

"Whatcha looking for?" Noel asked Abby.

"Chocolate chips," Abby said, her voice muffled by the fact that her head was stuffed into the cabinet.

Noel laughed. "I thought you were making peanut butter cookies."

"Aunt Abby said we could make peanut butter-chocolate chip cookies," Poppy said, looking more than pleased with herself.

"Got them!" Abby said and then reemerged with the chips held high over her head. She turned to Noel. "How is your pantry this stocked when you've only been fully moved in for three weeks?"

"Please, Abby. You know the Townsend girls can't go without their baked goods," Noel said with a laugh. "Besides, after all that moving, we needed to replenish our calories."

Abby cackled. "No kidding. My arms were sore for over a week." Clay and Abby, along with their sister Yvette and her husband Jacob, had helped them move in earlier in the month, while their other sister, Faith, had entertained the kids.

"I'm giving Olive the tour. I'll be back soon to help with the cookies," Noel said.

"We've got this," Abby said with a wave and turned her attention back to Poppy, who'd snatched the chocolate chips and was already tearing into the bag.

What could be better than this? Noel thought as she led Olive into the mud room and showed her the dog shower and grooming station they'd put in. "Now when Endora comes over and gets into the mud outside, we can just rinse her off."

"Mom!" Olive called. "We need a dog shower for Endora."

Abby called back, "When you make your first million, we'll put one in."

Olive rolled her eyes. "Mom thinks I'm gonna be some world-famous musician. I keep telling her that pianists just don't make that much."

"You never know. Maybe you'll start a band with your cousin Frankie and become world sensations." Frankie was Hope and Chad's adopted daughter, and she was quite the singer.

"A band? Yeah, right," Olive said, trying to play it cool, but Noel saw the interest sparking in her eyes.

"There are all kinds of possibilities for musicians. Just stay open about it, and your passion will find you," Noel said and then took her around the rest of the farmhouse to show her the changes they'd made.

"I can't believe this is the same house," Olive said, shaking her head when they finally ended up back in the living room. She turned to Daisy. "You even have your own bathroom!"

Not quite. It was a Jack-and-Jill bathroom that was between the girls' rooms, but they did each have their own private vanity area while the tub and toilet was a shared space right in the middle.

Noel left the two teenagers and went back into the kitchen to join the cookie-making party.

Flour coated her six-year-old from head to toe, and

there was a mound of it on the floor. Noel raised both eyebrows. "What happened here?"

Poppy's lower lip trembled when she haltingly said, "The flour container attacked me."

Abby hid a smirk and whispered, "It tipped over when she was pulling it out of the cabinet."

"Awe," Noel said, crouching down to look her daughter in the eye. "It's okay, love. I have more. Let's go get you cleaned up." She took her by the hand and led her into the downstairs bathroom where she got her washed up and then fetched her a clean shirt. "All better. Let's go finish helping Aunt Abby, okay?"

Poppy shook her head.

"No? But I thought you liked making cookies."

Poppy's voice was tentative, completely out of the norm for her, when she said, "She said Aunt Abby is next."

"Who said Abby is next? Next for what?" Noel frowned, suddenly worried. Poppy was a rambunctious little girl who was rarely afraid of anything. Something had happened in that kitchen, and it wasn't just a flour accident.

"The lady," Poppy said, glancing around as if looking for her.

"What lady, sweetheart?" Noel asked.

"The one with the pentacle necklace," she said.

Abby appeared in the bathroom doorway and Noel mouthed, *Do you know who she's talking about?*

Abby shook her head.

"Where did you see this lady with the pentacle?" Noel asked Poppy.

Her daughter scrunched up her face, concentrating, and then said, "In front of the stove. She just appeared and told me she saw a prem... premission?"

"Premonition?" Noel asked, trying to fill in the blanks.

Poppy nodded. "Yes, that. And then she said I'd be covered in flour."

"That happened right before the flour slipped from your fingers?" Abby asked.

"Yes." Poppy nodded furiously. "I don't know how she did it, but I'm sure it was her that dumped it on my head."

"Did this all happen when Aunt Abby was in the kitchen with you?" Noel asked, a ball of trepidation forming in the pit of her stomach.

"Yes. The lady was right behind Aunt Abby," Poppy said.

Noel didn't want to scare her daughter, but that sounded an awful lot like a ghost. She shared a knowing look with her sister. Neither of them was a medium, but seeing ghosts in Keating Hollow wasn't unheard of. In fact, Charlotte Pelsh, Abby's deceased best friend from high school, had shown herself to Abby once before.

"Tell me about this woman," Abby said. "What did she look like?"

"Tall. Skinny. Curly brown hair," Poppy said. "She was wearing a dress with boots and a long necklace with a pentacle on it."

"That doesn't really sound like someone we know," Noel said, wondering if the house was haunted by a previous resident. It was possible. It was an old farmhouse that was built a hundred years ago.

"Well," Abby said, sounding unconcerned. "It appears that she was just trying to warn you about the flour. If that's the case, then she was actually being helpful, right?"

"Not if she's the one who poured it on my head!" Poppy declared.

Noel chuckled. "You have a point, but it really sounds like the container just slipped."

Poppy crossed her arms over her chest and stuck her bottom lip out. "I don't think so."

"Okay, okay. It's possible. Are you ready to go finish making cookies?" Noel asked her with wink.

"The dough is ready to be scooped onto the cookie sheet," Abby added.

"All right." Poppy clutched Noel's hand and walked very slowly back to the kitchen. When they reached the doorway, Poppy stopped suddenly and scanned the room. Finally, she let out a sigh of relief. "The flour lady is gone."

"Good. Let's get those cookies done." Abby gestured for her to join her at the counter, and the two of them went to work while Noel dealt with the dirty dishes.

Just as Noel was finishing up and closing the dishwasher, she heard a startled cry from behind her. She whirled and froze as she took in the scene before her.

"That lady said Aunt Abby was next!" Poppy called and then started giggling.

Abby, who was standing at the pantry, was covered in flour. She blew out a breath, sending a puff of flour into the air and said, "I think Poppy's right. The lady is responsible for this."

"There she is," Poppy said, pointing into the dining room.

Noel followed her daughter's gaze and saw just an outline of a silver shadow before the image disappeared into the ether.

"Mommy? Is the lady a ghost?" Poppy asked, sounding more curious than scared.

"Yeah, honey. I think so. It looks like we've got a trickster sharing our house," Noel said.

"I'll get the sage," Abby said. "Just give me a second to clean up."

"Sounds like a plan," Noel said, her voice hitching as she tried to swallow a laugh. She leaned down and whispered to Poppy, "Abby's covered in so much flour she almost looks like a ghost herself."

Poppy covered her mouth as she giggled again.

"I heard that," Abby called over her shoulder. "Paybacks are hell!"

"I'm not scared!" Noel replied and then winked at Poppy. "Come on. We have flour to clean up."

As Noel was sweeping the kitchen, that silver outline appeared again, catching her eye. The outline shimmered and in the next few seconds, the tall woman with the long curly hair and pentacle necklace materialized for just a moment, her gaze piercing Noel.

Abby reappeared, catching her sister's attention. "I found the sage," Abby said, holding it up. "I had a bundle in my glovebox."

"Good." Noel turned back to the spirit, but she'd vanished. And Noel had a sinking suspicion that whoever it was wouldn't be deterred with a simple smudging. But they had to start somewhere. She put her broom away and turned her attention to Abby. "Ready?"

Abby pulled a lighter out of her pocket and together, they spread the sage around the house, inviting any and all spirits to move on.

CHAPTER 2

Drew Baker pulled into the long driveway that led to the newly remodeled farmhouse his family had just moved into a few weeks earlier. There were still plenty of projects he had on his list to improve the property, like prune the trees that lined the driveway and eventually wrap them with twinkle lights like his father-in-law had at the Townsend residence. He also wanted to build Noel a chicken coop. She'd been making noise about raising her own eggs. But most of all, he wanted to build a dedicated garden that was fenced to keep the wildlife out.

To say that he was knee-deep in domestic bliss with his wife and kids was an understatement. Here he was, dreaming about greenhouses and chicken coops. If only his teenage self could see him now.

He pulled his truck to a stop in front of the house, and as he opened the door, his daughter Poppy came flying out of the house, her arms raised as she called, "Daddy!"

"Hey, Poppy girl," he called back, his arms out, waiting for her. As soon as she reached him, he picked her up and spun her around, making her laugh with pure joy. This was the best part of his day. Coming home to the people he loved most in the world always took away the stress of his job. Even in a town as quaint and tranquil as Keating Hollow, being the town sheriff could really take it out of a person.

Drew spun Poppy around a few more times before planting a kiss on the top of her head and setting her back on the ground. The moment Poppy's feet hit the earth, she ran off again back into the house.

"Hey, handsome," Noel said from the front porch railing.

"Hey, beautiful." Drew strode up onto the porch, grabbed Noel by the waist, and dipped her back, making a big production of giving her a kiss.

She smiled up at him. "This is quite the greeting. You must be really excited to be off for the weekend. It's about time Keating Hollow hired a new officer. Are you nervous about leaving Adrian in charge?"

"Not at all. Adrian's only new to Keating Hollow, not police business." His new hire, Adrian Hunt, had come from Befana Bay and had quickly turned into Drew's right-hand deputy. When it came to protecting the citizens of Keating Hollow, Drew knew he could trust the man. Pauly Putzner, on the other hand, the former deputy sheriff, had just been demoted to school crossing guard and reprimanded after he'd gone on a three-day bender and accidentally fired his weapon, putting a hole in his neighbor's garage. To be honest, as much as Drew hated the circumstances, he was glad Pauly was no longer his second-in-command.

Drew pulled his wife back upright and then brushed a lock of her long auburn hair out of her eyes. "But yes, I'm excited about the weekend. Especially tonight. It's been forever since I've been able to take you out on a date."

"Date?" she asked, looking surprised. "Did we have plans?"

"We do now." He grabbed her hand and hauled her back into the house. "Why do you think Abby is still here?"

"Because she's baking cookies with Poppy?" Noel said, eyeing her sister who was standing in the doorway of the kitchen with suspicion. "Did you two set this up without telling me?"

Abby shrugged. "I wasn't going to pass up spending time with two of my favorite nieces."

Noel turned to Drew. "Daisy could've watched Poppy."

He shook his head. "Nope. Not overnight." He gave her a mischievous grin. "Go pack a bag. We have reservations."

His wife blinked up at him, shock in her pretty blue eyes. "You're kidding, right?"

"Nope. It's all planned," he said and then frowned. "Unless you don't want to. Did you have plans I didn't know about?"

"No, no plans." Noel shook her head. "Just surprised and…" She glanced at Abby. "Clay is fine with you staying over? What about Lynette and little George?" she asked, referring to Abby's other two children.

"Grandma asked for an overnight with the kids, and Clay is busy at the brewery. He said something about maintenance on the tanks." She pumped her eyebrows. "Honestly, this is more of a mini vacation for me. You know George is a little ball of energy. And since Olive was already spending the evening with Daisy, it all worked out perfectly."

"Okay then. If you're sure."

"I'm sure," Abby said. "Poppy and I have big plans that include a blanket fort, streaming the Taylor Swift concert, and making popcorn if the cookies run out. You two go have fun and don't worry about us at all."

Noel beamed at her sister. "You're the best." Then

she bit down on her bottom lip and asked, "You'll call if anything unusual happens?"

"Of course," Abby said, sounding offended her sister even felt she had to ask.

"Unusual?" Drew asked, glancing between them in confusion. Noel was obviously excited about a night out. He just didn't understand why she was acting so hesitant. He'd thought she'd jump at the chance to unwind for an evening. He peered at Noel's frown. "You're worried about something. What is it?"

She let out a long sigh. "It appears that our dream home came with a ghost."

"That's not really a surprise, is it?" Drew asked. "It's an old house. The chances of a spirit hanging around were pretty good, right?"

"Yep," Abby and Noel said at the same time.

Noel chuckled softly and shook her head as she and Abby grinned at each other. Then she turned back to Drew. "I shouldn't be shocked about the ghost. It is Keating Hollow after all, but if that smudging Abby and I performed didn't work and she starts dumping flour on *my* head, we're gonna need to bring in reinforcements ASAP."

"Flour?" Drew raised one eyebrow. "Why do I get the feeling I'm missing something?"

"Because the ghost got both me and Poppy," Abby

said. "But don't worry. I've got this handled. You two go on and have a nice evening."

Drew finally understood why Noel was being so cagey. Having a docile ghost that just hung around was one thing, but an active one was entirely another. "Is this something we need to be worried about? Maybe we should cancel and stay home."

"No!" Abby called over her shoulder as she disappeared back into the house. "Get out of here before I force you out."

Noel laughed at her sister and then stepped in to wrap her arms around Drew. "She's right. Let's not talk ourselves out of this rare opportunity for a little alone time. The smudging probably did the trick. If not, the worst thing that's happened was a little flour mess. Abby can handle things, but she'll call us if anything gets out of hand." Then she paused and stared up at Drew, her expression softening. "How long have you been planning this night out?"

Pulling Noel in closer, Drew gave her a little smile and said, "A while."

"Drew!" She reached up and placed both hands on his cheeks. "Why are you being so evasive?"

He chuckled, loving it when he riled her up. Her inner fire was what had attracted him to her in the first place. "A few months. The remodel took so much out of us in both time and resources, and while I think it was more than worth it, we both deserve a break. Now come on. Let's get dressed for dinner and pack something to wear in the morning." His lips twitched into a mischievous grin. "But don't worry about tonight. Once I get you alone, you won't be wearing much for long."

Her eyes flashed with desire. And then without a word, she grabbed his hand and hauled him upstairs.

Drew was busy shoving his toothbrush into his toiletry bag when he heard Noel's phone start to ring. He didn't think anything of it when she refused the call, but when she immediately started texting, he frowned her direction. "Who is it?"

"Oh, just Bianca at the inn. She's having trouble finding the extra coffee pods." She shoved her phone into her pocket and went back to packing.

Bianca was the manager Noel had hired for the inn six months ago. She was the reason Noel was able to take more time off these days. For the first time since she'd opened the place, Noel was able to leave the day-to-day details to her staff while she managed special events and filled in for vacations and sick days instead of having to actually run the front desk. It was the perfect situation she'd been working toward for years.

"She didn't know where the coffee pods were?" Drew asked.

"They were hiding in the pantry. It happens," Noel

said with a shrug as she disappeared into the walk-in closet.

Drew nodded, but for some odd reason, he'd just gotten the feeling that Noel wasn't being completely honest with him. Like she was hiding something. But why would she lie about coffee pods?

He went back to packing, and when his wife stepped out of the closet a few minutes later wearing a gorgeous red dress that was cut just right to show off her curves, all thoughts of coffee pods vanished from his mind. Letting out a low whistle, he walked over to her, unable to keep his hands to himself. "If this house wasn't full of kids and your sister, that dress would be on the floor in ten seconds flat."

She pressed her hands to his chest and kissed him so thoroughly that they were both breathless when they pulled apart. She gazed up at him with a soft smile and said, "The wait will only make it that much sweeter."

Drew let out a low growl, grabbed their bags and her hand, and led her out the door.

CHAPTER 3

Noel's phone buzzed in her pocket for the fifth time in five minutes, making her regret her life choices. If Henry, the manager of Woodlines, texted her one more time about the menu for Drew's surprise birthday party, she was going to lose her mind. What was so hard about a buffet that had both seafood and vegan options? She'd already told him that the only requirement was crab legs, since those were Drew's favorite.

"Is that Bianca again?" Drew asked as he dipped his spoon into his lobster bisque. They were at an upscale restaurant in the quaint town of Trinidad, California, enjoying their appetizers. Drew had booked them a gorgeous short-term rental that had a view of the ocean from nearly every window.

"Yeah, problem with a double booking." Noel jumped up, clutching her phone. "I'll just give her a call and be right back. I'm sorry. I know it's not quite the romantic dinner you'd planned."

"It's all right," he said, but Noel couldn't help but notice the tick of his jaw, indicating that he was irritated.

Join the club, buddy. If his party wasn't next week, she'd completely ignore Henry until she could go see him in person and give him a piece of her mind. Texting and calling multiple times on a Friday night, especially after she'd said she was out of town, was just unacceptable. Once she was outside, she returned his call.

"Thank goodness," Henry said, sounding stressed. "I need to know If anyone is allergic to garlic."

"What?" Noel kicked a rock, sending it skittering right toward a couple who was headed her way. "Sorry," she whispered and gave them an embarrassed grimace.

"Watch it, lady," the woman said, careful to step over the rock.

They hurried down the sidewalk, their heads bent together, and the entire exchange only made her angrier at Henry. "Seriously? That's why you're blowing up my phone?" she said, trying and failing to keep her voice down. "I already told you that the only issue is that we have a couple of vegans coming. No allergies. Garlic is fine."

"Oh, good," he said, letting out a sigh of relief. "My cousin has an aversion to garlic, and if she gets even a tiny bit of it, she spends all night on the toilet. I wanted to make sure that doesn't happen at Drew's party."

Noel was so incredulous she was speechless. After a long moment, she sucked in a deep breath and said, "Henry, I am out of town, enjoying a nice dinner with Drew. Do not call or text me again for at least twenty-four hours, understand?"

"But what if I have more questions? If I don't get this menu done tonight, I fear things won't be ready for his party next weekend. There's planning and ordering and test dishes. It doesn't just happen in one day, Noel."

Noel wondered why she hadn't just planned to have the party at her dad's house. They could have had a low-key potluck. No doubt her sisters would have helped her. But it wouldn't have been the fancy celebration she'd had in mind.

"Make some executive decisions, Henry. As long as there are crab legs and something for the vegans, I'm good. Okay?"

"What about dessert? Do you need a cake?" he asked, sounding panicked.

"No!" Noel pressed a hand to her forehead and debated canceling altogether.

"Oh, right. I see here that you have that covered," Henry said. "Okay, I'll email you the final menu."

"Fine. I'm turning my phone off for the rest of the weekend, so don't bother calling until Monday."

Henry let out a bark of laughter. "You're so funny, Noel. Good one."

"I'm not—"

"I'll talk to you tomorrow," he said and then the line went dead.

Noel let out a growl of frustration and nearly threw her phone when it buzzed again. But when she saw Abby's name flash on the screen, she rushed to answer it. "What's wrong?"

"Nothing," Abby said with a soft chuckle. "Good goddess, Noel, you're acting like a new mom with how nervous you are."

"It's not that. Henry keeps calling and texting while we're trying to have dinner. I keep throwing Bianca under the bus as an excuse. By the time the night's over, Drew is probably going to think that my inn manager is the most incompetent person in Keating Hollow."

"Oh, honey," Abby said with a soft chuckle. "I'm sure he'll just think she's having one of those nights. But if you want, I'll call Henry and tell him to call me if he has any more questions."

"No, don't do that. You'll spend the rest of the night

fielding his inane inquiries," Noel said. "You don't want to invite that. Trust me."

"But if it keeps him from ruining your date night, then I'm more than willing. Olive and Daisy are busy making playlists, and Poppy has passed out in the blanket fort. It's just me and the pups, hanging out while I watch *Practical Magic* for the eighty-seventh time," Abby said.

Noel sighed. "That actually sounds like heaven."

"Noel!" Abby admonished. "You're out with your husband… alone for the first time in months. You do not want to be here watching movies with the dogs."

"No, no," Noel said with a bark of laughter. "You're absolutely right. I wouldn't trade my time with Drew for anything. But your evening does sound like a nice break. Don't listen to me. Henry is just stressing me out. I hate having to make up stuff so I don't ruin the surprise."

"Give me his number. I'll make sure he doesn't call or text you again for the rest of the weekend," Abby insisted.

"He shouldn't, but… Yeah, okay. I'll text it to you as soon as we get off the phone." Noel wrapped her arm across her body, rubbing her arm as a gust of wind chilled her. "Now, is everything okay there? The girls aren't giving you a hard time, are they?"

"Of course not," Abby scoffed. "They love their Aunt Abby."

Noel snorted. "Sure they do. But if they think they can get away with something, there's no telling what they'll get up to."

Abby laughed. "I have three kids, remember? I'm well aware. I only called to tell you that there's no sign of the ghost and to find out where you keep the good ice cream."

It was Noel's turn to laugh. "You really just called for the ice cream, didn't you? You never could pass up chocolate caramel swirl."

"Absolutely. Now that Poppy's passed out, I figured I deserved a treat, but I didn't find it in the back of your freezer." There was no mistaking the pout in Abby's tone.

"You're a piece of work," Noel teased. "Calling me to find the expensive ice cream while I'm on my date. You should be ashamed."

"And yet, I'm not at all. Where is it, Noel? I know it's here somewhere."

After cackling at her sister, Noel barely composed herself before she said, "It's in the freezer in the container labeled *Chili*. The girls are never gonna look there."

"You. Are. Brilliant. Gotta go. The ice cream is calling my name. See you in the morning."

After Noel ended the call, she quickly texted Henry's number to Abby and then silenced her phone. With Abby on the case, Noel felt better about ignoring the man for the rest of the night.

"Okay, crisis averted," Noel said when she rejoined Drew back at their table.

"Do I even want to know?" he asked, picking up his wine glass and taking a sip.

"No. Just a reservation crisis. All fixed. She promises she won't call again unless the place is burning down."

"I hope you told her that if such an unfortunate event occurs, she should just call Yvette."

Noel smirked. Her sister, Yvette, was a powerful fire witch. She was, in fact, the one to call in case of a fire emergency. "She knows. Now, where were we?"

Her husband pointed at her tuna tartare. "Appetizers, remember?"

"Of course I do. I meant, where were we in our conversation? You said something about heading over to the farm supply place tomorrow when we get back into town. Whatcha need? More fencing supplies?"

"Oh, that. Well…" he said slowly. "It's spring, and I heard they have chickens in stock. And I thought—"

"Chickens?" Noel exclaimed, excitement filling her soul. For as long as she could remember, she'd wanted a mini farm. That had all been put on hold when she'd purchased the inn, but now that they had the farmhouse and the surrounding land, she'd made some noise about chickens, but Drew hadn't shown much interest. "You want to get chickens?"

He laughed. "*You* want to get chickens. I figured we'd pick up the supplies to build that chicken coop and check out the chicks to see which type you want."

Noel reached across the table and squeezed both of his hands. "You're going to build me a chicken coop?"

"Your dad said he'd help. The farm supply has some kits that we can just pick up and assemble in a day or so. If you're still interested, then I thought we'd work on that on Sunday."

Squealing with excitement, Noel jumped up and ran over to the other side of the table and hugged her husband, pressing her cheek to the top of his head. "You, Mr. Baker, are the best husband in the world."

"I know," he said with a wink and then pulled her down so that she was sitting in his lap.

"Drew," she said, grinning. "I don't think this is the appropriate place for this." But instead of sliding off his lap, she leaned in and gave him a slow, lingering kiss.

Her husband tightened his grip on her, deepening the kiss, making her feel as if she were the most desirable woman in the world.

"Ah-hem," a man said, hovering over them.

Noel pulled back and felt her face flush with heat when she looked up at the gentleman who was wearing a suit and looked like he might be the manager. He was staring down at them, judgment written all over his face. "I'm going to have to ask you to take your seat, ma'am."

Ma'am? Noel thought as she watched a waiter appear from behind the man and place their dinners on the table. She wasn't a ma'am yet, was she? Just because she'd be forty in a few short years, that didn't make her a ma'am. At least not in her book.

Drew squeezed her one last time before she took her own seat, and then he cleared his throat as he met the manager's piercing gaze. "My apologies." He gave the man a knowing smile. "It's our first night out alone without the kids in months. I'm sure you understand."

The judgment disappeared from the manager's face, and he relented with a smirk. "Sure do." He glanced at Noel and then back at Drew. Nodding his approval, he said, "It looks like you have a good night ahead of you. Just do me a favor and keep it PG until you're behind closed doors."

"You got it, Chief," Drew said, giving the man a little salute.

After the manager left, Drew leaned across the table and whispered, "I'm headed to the restroom." He raised one suggestive eyebrow. "Care to meet me in there in two minutes?"

Noel let out a bark of laughter. "Are you trying to

get us arrested, Sheriff Baker? I can't imagine that would be a good look for your career."

He shrugged. "The guy said to keep it behind closed doors. I wasn't suggesting a public spectacle."

"You're crazy," Noel said, unable to stop her giggling. "As much as I'd love a quickie in the restroom, I was hoping to take my time tonight." She let her gaze drop to his lips and then lower as she imagined an entire night with him, with zero interruptions. "I wouldn't want to ruin the anticipation."

Heat flared in Drew's eyes, and his voice was husky when he said, "Then we better eat fast because I'm not sure I can wait that much longer."

Noel grabbed her fork and dug in.

They ate in record time and then rushed back to their rental. The moment they were through the door, Drew pressed Noel against the wall and attacked her neck as if he were a starving man.

The thrill of knowing they had the entire place to themselves, that no kids would walk in on them, had her yanking on his clothes, desperate to feel every inch of him right there in the entry.

"It's been too long, Noel," he said between kisses, his hands roaming down her sides until they settled on her backside.

Noel moaned her agreement as she started unbuttoning his shirt. When she went to push it off his shoulders, Drew spun her and started walking her backward toward the bedroom. Articles of his clothing were left in a trail down the short hallway and into the bedroom. By the time they reached the bed, all that was left was his jeans. Noel stripped him naked first, and then Drew took his turn. Her dress landed with a soft rustle of fabric on the hardwood, causing her phone that was in one of her pockets to skitter toward Drew's feet.

The phone lit up with a text, just as they both went for it. Drew got to it first and frowned when he saw the text. "Who's HW, and what's happening on Friday?"

Noel glanced at the screen of her phone and sure enough, there was a text from Henry. *Everything's set. See you Friday at seven.*

Son of a... crap! Noel took the phone from her husband, turned the screen off, and set it on the nightstand. "Just a guest at the inn. They're planning a family event."

It was a normal statement. Something she'd said to Drew dozens of times since she'd taken over the event planning at the inn. But she must have sounded off, because Drew gave her an assessing look. The one he gave the girls when he was sure they weren't telling the whole truth.

"Forget the inn stuff," Noel said, running her hands

over his chest. "We have more important things to think about."

His light green eyes darkened with heat as he stared down at her naked body.

"Drew?" she whispered softly.

"Yes, love?"

"Make love to me."

All thoughts fled as her husband swiftly lifted her into his arms and laid her on the bed. And as he climbed over the top of her, he said, "I thought you'd never ask."

CHAPTER 4

The brilliant spring sun shone in Drew's eyes as he walked up behind his wife and slipped his arms around her.

Noel jumped slightly as her phone slipped from her hand and landed in the dirt.

He chuckled and reached for it at the same time as she did. Their heads knocked together, and they both let out a cry of pain as they came up, each of them holding their noggins with one hand.

"Ouch," Noel said, rubbing her head.

"Sorry about that." Drew reached down and picked up her phone, noting it was yet another text from her assistant. "Is that work again?"

"It's just Bianca letting me know that everything

went smoothly this weekend," Noel said, tucking the phone into her pocket.

"Everything except Friday night," Drew said, sounding grumpy even to his own ears.

"Uh, right. How could I forget?" Noel flushed and glanced away, looking uneasy. "Besides that."

Instantly, Drew felt terrible for bringing it up. Bianca was supposed to make Noel's life less stressful. Noel certainly didn't need his judgment when they were clearly still working through the kinks. Besides, he was sure they'd settle in soon enough and things would go smoother in the future. Wrapping his arm around her shoulders, he pointed to the area off to the right of the house, behind the garage. "Last chance for input on where the chicken coop should go. Lin and I were thinking that might be the best place."

"That looks good to me." She beamed up at him. "I can't wait for the chicks to get old enough to get acquainted with their new home."

On the way back into town the day before, Drew and Noel had stopped at the farm supply store and picked up the ready-to-build chicken coop. They'd also scooped up about a dozen chicks as well as everything they needed for their little flock to thrive. Now Drew, along with his father-in-law, was getting ready to build the coop, despite the fact the chicks would be living in their utility room for the next five to six weeks before they were ready to move out on their own.

"That will come soon enough." Drew kissed his wife on the cheek before glancing at his watch. "Your dad will be here in about an hour. I'm going to get the kit laid out so we're ready to go when he gets here."

"Sounds good." Noel smiled up at him, her eyes alight with happiness. "Let me know if you need help."

"I'm helping Daddy," Poppy said, appearing out of nowhere.

Drew glanced down at his youngest daughter. "Is that right?"

"Yep." She held up her kid-sized pink hammer. After following Drew around while he fixed various things on the house, they'd gotten Poppy her own set of age-appropriate tools for Christmas the previous year, and she loved using them when she was helping Daddy.

"Excellent," Drew said. "Come with me. I have just the job for you."

Noel raised her eyebrows in question at him.

He just winked and took his daughter by the hand. She skipped along with him, swinging their hands wildly as she chattered about the twin fawns that had visited them earlier that morning.

"I wanted to name them Bambi and Thumper, but Daisy said we needed something more original. So I decided Pebbles and Bamm-Bamm was better."

Drew chuckled, unsurprised by her choice. She'd recently found the old *Flintstones* cartoon on streaming and watched religiously every day after school. "Good choice." They entered the small barn, and Drew led her to the workbench. "Do you want to help me nail these directional markers to this post?"

"Mommy and I painted these last week!" she said, beaming up at him. Noel had painted different destinations onto boards that had arrows at one end. There were two for other witchy towns. One read *Befana Bay, WA, 590 miles* and the other, *Salem, MA, 3194 miles*. And then there were ones that just listed the distance to other places in Keating Hollow, like *Grandpa Lin's, 1 mile* and *Incantation Café, 11 miles*.

"Yep. Now we're putting it together, and then we'll find a place out front to hammer it into the ground," he explained. "What do you say?"

She bounced up and down. "Do I get to hammer the nails?"

"Yep," he said seriously as he grabbed a few nails and got one started. He held the nail with his thumb and forefinger. "Now go ahead, but be careful. Don't hit Daddy's fingers."

"Okay." Poppy bit down on her lip in concentration and carefully tapped at the nail.

"Try just a little bit harder," Drew coaxed.

Poppy looked up at him with worry in her big blue eyes. "I don't want to miss and hit your fingers."

"I appreciate that," he said, ruffling her hair affectionately. "But you're going to need to give it a little more muscle or that nail isn't going to move, and we'll be here all day."

"Okay," she said, sounding skeptical. But she didn't hesitate to wrap both hands around the handle of her hammer and then give it a good thwack. The nail moved about a half inch, causing her to squeal with delight. "I did it!"

"Great job!" He oversaw her hammering for the next few minutes until her interest waned, and then he finished the job himself while she wandered around the barn, testing out names for their new chicks.

"Layer Swift," she said and giggled.

"That's clever, Poppy," Drew said, cleaning up the workstation.

"Oh, I like Little Red Riding Hen." Poppy clapped her hands together and jumped up and down.

Drew couldn't help but laugh.

"That's it! Princess Lay-a! Can we use that one, Daddy?"

"Of course, pumpkin." He turned to eye his daughter. "Who helped you come up with those?"

She just stared back at him, an innocent look on her face.

He didn't believe for one second that she'd pulled those puns out of nowhere, but he was willing to let her have her secrets. "Come on." He held his hand out to her. "Let's get this sign in the ground, and then Daddy has to get to work."

"Okay." She skipped alongside him, and after she approved the location for the sign, she stepped back and let him hammer it in the ground.

"Done," Drew said. "What do you think?" He gestured to the wooden sign.

"Clara's a good name," she said, staring past him.

Drew spun, looking to see what she was looking at or who she was speaking to, but when he didn't see anything but the driveway, he asked, "For a chicken? What about Amelia Egghart?"

"No, her name's Clara," she said, shaking her head and then rolling her eyes at him.

"Right. Well, I'm sure you can name one of them Clara if you want to."

Poppy shrugged and followed him back to the house. She immediately ran into the living room, where her sister was playing with her dog, Buffy.

Drew walked over to his wife and gave her a kiss on the temple. "Our daughter has some good names picked out for the chicks. I'm guessing you two came up with Layer Swift together?"

Noel's eyebrows shot up as she gave him a half smile and shook her head no. "Not me. Must've been Daisy."

"Clever girls we've got there."

Chuckling, Noel nodded and went back to working on lunch. "I'll call you when this is ready."

"Thanks." Drew took off out to the barn and spent the next thirty minutes unloading the pieces of the chicken coop and laying them out in the section of the yard he and Lin had chosen. He was just about done when he walked back into the barn for a tool and was stopped in his tracks, as suddenly, what appeared to be an entire bag of seed was unceremoniously poured on his head.

He let out a startled cry of dismay and then just stood there, looking up at the loft just above him, trying to see the culprit. "Poppy? Daisy? Is that you?"

Silence.

He ground his teeth together and took a deep breath, trying to get his temper under control before he climbed the ladder to the loft. When he reached the top, he glanced around and spotted the culprit. "Poppy?" He glared at his youngest daughter, who was sitting against the wall, her eyes wide. "What do you think you're doing?"

She shook her head, and her bottom lip trembled.

He stifled a sigh and held out his hand. "Come on. You know you're not supposed to be up here."

Without a word, she scrambled to the edge and let him help her down. Once they were on solid ground again, he turned to face her with his arms crossed over his chest. "Explain yourself, young lady."

Poppy audibly swallowed. But she met his eyes and said, "Clara did it."

"Clara?" he echoed, confused. "What do you mean? Who's Clara?"

"The ghost. She did it, Daddy," Poppy said.

"Don't lie, Poppy," Daisy said and clucked her tongue as she appeared in the doorway of the barn. She turned to look at Drew. "I was in my room and could see Poppy through the barn window. I don't know why she did it, but she's the one who poured that seed on you."

Drew let out a long-suffering sigh. "Poppy, go inside and go to your room."

"But—" his youngest child started.

He held his hand up. "We'll talk about this later. Right now I have seed to clean up before your grandfather gets here."

"Too late," Lincoln Townsend said as he walked into the barn. He paused at the pile of grass seed, took one look at Drew, and had to stifle an amused smile.

Don't even think about it, Drew thought as he stared down his father-in-law. If Poppy knew she'd tickled her grandfather's funny bone, she'd only be more inclined to push the boundaries of what was acceptable behavior.

"Well, looks like you could use some help, so I'll get on that." Lincoln tipped his hat to Drew's daughters and then went to get a shovel.

"Daisy, take your sister inside," Drew said.

"Sure, Dad."

Drew's heart melted a little, just as it always did when she called him that. Technically, Daisy was his stepdaughter, but he'd never seen her that way. To him, she was just Daisy, and he was damned proud to be her parent. "But Daisy, leave the lectures to me and your mother, okay?"

Daisy's smiled slipped slightly, and Drew knew she'd been looking forward to admonishing Poppy. It was what big sisters lived for. "Fine."

Once the two girls were out of earshot, Lin started chuckling.

"Don't you start," Drew said, unable to keep his own lips from twitching with amusement.

"It's never a dull moment with a house full of girls, is it?" Lincoln asked as he scooped up a pile of seed.

"No. But it's not nice to make fun of your favorite son-in-law either. You know that, right?" Drew asked dryly.

"Oh? Was I making fun of Clay? I didn't realize," Lin said with a smirk.

"Ha-ha. Very funny." Drew rolled his eyes but then started laughing as he got to work with Lincoln.

CHAPTER 5

"It's not fair. I really did see a ghost," Poppy insisted, her face scrunched up with petulance. It was Monday afternoon, and Poppy had come home from school upset because she hadn't been allowed to go to her friend's house for the afternoon.

Noel sat on the edge of her daughter's bed and brushed her curls back gently. "I'm not questioning that you did, sweetie. But Daisy saw you kick the grass seed bag over and then lift it so it poured all over Daddy's head."

Poppy stared down at her hands that were clutched in her lap and said nothing.

It was a sure sign that Daisy had been telling the truth about what she'd seen. Poppy was a fighter, but only when she was wrongly accused of something.

Lying wasn't one of her strong suits. But that didn't explain *why* Poppy decided to dump the seed out. It had probably just been a precocious impulse like kids were prone to have every now and then. But she'd still have to pay the price for misbehaving.

"Okay, show me where you saw the ghost," Noel said and held her hand out to Poppy.

But her daughter shook her head. "I'm not going back into the barn. It's too scary."

"Too scary?" Noel frowned. "Honey, what aren't you telling me?"

"I don't want to see the ghost."

Noel's heart started to beat faster as her pulse sped up. "She scared you?"

Poppy nodded and then flung herself at her mother, grabbing onto her neck with such force that Noel had to gently pull back just so she could breathe.

"You're okay," Noel whispered as she ran her hand up and down her daughter's back. "I promise."

Poppy pressed her head against Noel's shoulder and just nodded.

"Hey." Noel repositioned herself so that she was leaning against the headboard and then pulled her daughter so that she was sitting sideways in her lap. "Why don't we go feed the chicks and clean up their area? Then we can have a cookie snack as a reward."

When Poppy just tightened her grip, Noel knew she

had to do something about the ghost, or her daughter was going to be paralyzed in her own home.

"Come on," Noel said softly and gently guided her daughter to get up. "Layer Swift is probably missing you."

Poppy clung to Noel's hand, but at the mention of her favorite chick, she appeared to be motivated to go see her.

When they got to the utility room, Noel couldn't help pausing and taking a long look just to make sure there wasn't any ghost hanging around. When she was satisfied their only company was a flock of chicks, the tension in her shoulders faded.

"Don't forget to change the water," Noel told Poppy as she headed for the yellow chick with a white cap on its head that was standing in the corner making noises, while five other chicks gathered around to watch her. "You certainly named that one correctly, Poppy. Layer Swift always seems to be in the spotlight."

Poppy ignored her and went to watch the show just like the other chicks were.

By the time Noel was done cleaning up the mess and making sure the chicks had what they needed to eat, Poppy had Layer Swift in her arms and was cooing at the chick. It might have been the most adorable thing she'd witnessed in ages.

Finally, Poppy put Layer Swift back down with her

fellow chicks, looked at Noel with a cheeky smile, and asked, "Do we have any cookies?"

Noel was so relieved that her daughter seemed to have bounced back that she grinned and said, "Absolutely. What kind do you want? Chocolate chip?"

Poppy nodded, and before Noel could even answer, Poppy made a beeline to the cookie jar, took out four cookies, and then offered one to Noel.

"Thanks," Noel said. "Who are the others for?" As soon as the words were out of her mouth, she wanted to stuff them back in. The only other person in the house was Daisy. Surely the extra cookie wasn't for the ghost, was it?

"Me and Daisy," she said, clutching the cookies with a death grip as if someone was going to take them away from her.

"Just you and your sister?" Noel asked, eyeing her with suspicion.

Poppy suddenly broke and confessed. "I was going to eat one with you and then one with Daisy. But I'll share it with her."

Noel tossed her head back and laughed. Yep, her daughter was definitely feeling better.

"Okay, that's fair." Noel walked with Poppy to Daisy's room. She knocked a few times until Daisy finally came to the door as she yanked out her earbuds.

"What's wrong?" Daisy asked, looking between her mother and her little sister. "Did something happen?"

"We brought cookies," Noel said brightly.

Daisy looked down at her little sister. "That was sweet."

"This one's for you." Poppy held out the one in her left hand. Then she quickly added, "We have to share the extra one."

"Sweet." Daisy sat on her floor in front of her computer and patted the carpet. "Sit next to me and let's watch something. Your choice."

Noel gave her oldest daughter a grateful smile. Somehow she'd known that Noel wanted her to keep an eye on Poppy.

"I'm going to go take care of some gardening. I shouldn't be too long," Noel said and then whispered to Daisy to keep Poppy inside so she wasn't subjected to any spells that might be cast.

Daisy gave her a questioning look, no doubt wondering what spells her mother might be casting if her daughters had to stay inside, but when Noel shook her head, Daisy shrugged and said, "Okay."

"Thanks, love." Noel kissed them both on the top of their heads before walking out and disappearing down the stairs. On her way out, she grabbed her pentacle, the sage, and a small book of curses she'd collected over the years. If anything went wrong while expelling the ghost in her barn, she'd be ready.

~

THERE WAS a chill in the air when Noel stepped out the back door of the farmhouse. Clouds had formed, and it looked like they might get an evening rain shower. Normally she'd welcome the weather. The fresh scent of the redwoods right after the rain always comforted her. It reminded her of stormy nights spent in front of the fireplace when she was a child. Her dad would let them make s'mores in the living room, and they'd camp out as if they really were sleeping in the woods. But this evening all she felt was eerie dread.

There was something unsettling in the air, and in that moment, Noel knew without a doubt that her baby girl had experienced something she never should have been subjected to.

Noel squared her shoulders and went straight into the barn.

I wondered when you'd come for me.

The voice came from the loft, and pure adrenaline coursed through Noel's veins as she looked up and spotted a silvery figure staring down at her. "Who are you and what do you want from us?"

I'm Clara, the ghost said, her voice high like a

tinkling bell. She darted from the edge of the loft, moving out of sight.

"You're not welcome here anymore, Clara." Noel's voice was strong and full of conviction. "It's time to leave."

It definitely is, the ghost said from right behind Noel.

An ice-cold chill ran up Noel's spine, causing a full-body shudder. But Noel stood her ground, knowing the spirit was trying to weaken her defenses. Most ghosts in Keating Hollow were harmless, but every now and then one would show up with an agenda and they weren't afraid to use anyone they could to complete their unfinished business. Those were the ones who could be dangerous.

"Go then," Noel said.

I'll be happy to, Clara said, her voice a whisper in the fading light.

Unease crawled through Noel, and suddenly she wished she'd called Harlow Thane, the town's most well-known medium, to help her banish Clara. Harlow was a professional who had more experience than anyone at exorcising ghosts. She slid her book of curses into her front pocket and reached for her phone. Just as she pulled it out of her pocket, an invisible force grabbed it, and the phone went flying across the barn, crashing into the wall. It fell with a loud *thunk* on the concrete floor. She prayed her phone case had kept it from cracking.

"Hey!" Noel cried. "That was uncalled for."

I don't think so, Clara said, appearing right in front of Noel in solid form. *You see, electronics zap my energy. No phones allowed. At least not yet.*

Noel took a step back, fear triggering her fight-or-flight mode. Her head was telling her to get the hell out of there, but with her daughters in the house, she could not take the risk that Clara would follow her. She had to do something about her *now*.

Where are you going, Noel? The spirit asked, moving back into Noel's personal space.

"Away from the creepy spirit who looks like she wants to eat my soul," Noel said, running her thumb over the pentacle in her hand and concentrating on the book of curses tucked into her jeans pocket. She knew the incantation she wanted; she just didn't know the exact wording.

You think that's cute? Clara asked, her lips morphing into a snarl. *Wait until you're trapped in this plane of hell, then we'll see how you really feel about things.*

"Is that a threat?" Noel demanded.

Clara stared her down. *Yes.*

Then the spirit shot forward, her hands outstretched as if she were going for Noel's neck.

Noel swung the pentacle she was holding from the

chain, slicing through the spirit and creating an open wound that spilled silver.

Clara stared down at it with her mouth ajar, clearly shocked that Noel was able to slow her down.

It was just the opening Noel needed. Using her air magic, she pictured the curse book in her mind's eye and imagined it open right in front of her to the page she needed. The book flew out of her pocket and flipped open to page 29. The curse was titled *Binding a Spirit*, but it was written in Latin.

She scanned the curse and started to call out, "Dimitiss spir—"

Before Noel was able to finish the chant, Clara's hand wrapped around Noel's neck, forcing her into silence. She tried to claw for the spirit's grip, but her arms wouldn't move. Nor would her mouth. There was no fighting for her life or her voice. The spirit had complete control of Noel. She was powerless to do anything, even when every cell in her body begged her to fight.

She just couldn't. Her power was neutralized and so were her limbs. She felt as if she'd been given a full-body anesthetic, and the only part of her that functioned was her mind. But if she didn't break free immediately, she was going to lose that, too.

Poppy's and Daisy's faces popped into her mind, and as hot tears stung her eyes, she quickly pushed the images away. Thinking about her daughters now would only make everything worse. She didn't know if Clara would come for them next or—

I don't want your kids, Clara scoffed. *I want you.* The spirit stared straight into Noel's eyes as if she were trying to find her very soul, and then suddenly, a self-satisfied smile claimed Clara's lips and the spirit walked right into Noel's body.

A fire ignited deep inside of Noel, and the pain was so intense she thought that she'd burn to ash from the inside out. But as quickly as the fire appeared, it vanished, and Noel's insides turned to ice. She fell to her knees, unable to hold herself up as she gasped for air. "What are you doing to me?"

Taking what I need.

Noel's world faded into blackness as she felt herself slipping away into nothing.

When she woke, after what felt like only seconds later, she was parking her car behind Woodlines in downtown Keating Hollow.

What's happening? she tried to say, but the words wouldn't come out.

"Oh, you're back," Clara said, only the high-pitched, tinkling voice came out of Noel's lips.

And in that one horrifying moment, Noel knew Clara had managed to possess her.

CHAPTER 6

*D*rew strode into his quiet house, wondering where everyone had gone. Noel's SUV hadn't been parked out front and the living room was cast in long shadows from the setting sun.

"Anyone home?" he called out as he walked into the kitchen, flipping on the lights.

"We're here," Daisy said, standing in the kitchen doorway, holding Poppy's hand.

"Hey. Where's your mom?" Drew reached for the coffee pot, desperately needing a hit of caffeine after his long day at the station. It'd been one of those days where everything that could go wrong had. His deputy had been in a fender bender in the cruiser, the computers were down, and there was an altercation down by the river that had resulted in Drew getting an elbow to the eye. If he didn't get ice on it, he'd for sure look like a raccoon in the morning.

"She, um, went to town, I think?" Daisy offered, her voice so tentative that Drew frowned.

"You seem unsure. Didn't she tell you where she was going?" Drew took down a mug, impatient for his coffee to brew.

"No," Poppy said, shaking her head. "She just left."

Unease curled in his gut, and his muscles tensed. That unease he often felt on the job when something wasn't right washed over him, making the hair stand up on his arms. If there was one thing he knew about Noel, it was that she would never just leave her children without so much as a word.

Something was wrong.

Seriously wrong.

He pulled out his phone and tapped her number. It rang four times before her voice mail kicked in. He immediately checked her location and furrowed his brow when her phone didn't show up at all. Maybe her battery had died? When was the last time his wife had let that happen? Never, as far as he knew, not when she had a business to run and two daughters to care for. Drew met Daisy's worried gaze. "How long ago did she leave?"

"About an hour." Daisy bit down on her lower lip as she glanced down at her sister and then back at Drew.

After repeating that cycle a few times, Drew got the message that she wanted to tell him something but didn't want to say it in front of Poppy.

"Hey, sweetheart," he said, holding his hand out to Poppy. "Can you do me a favor? Can you go put a sweater on Buffy? It's supposed to be cooler tonight, and I don't want her to be cold when I take her out." The sweater wasn't necessary, but it would keep Poppy occupied long enough for Drew to find out what was on Daisy's mind.

"Okay." Poppy disappeared down the hallway, calling, "Come on Buffy. It's time to play dress up!"

Drew turned his attention to Daisy. "What's going on?"

She hurried to him and wrapped her arms around his waist. With her head buried in his chest, she said, "I'm worried. Mom was acting weird before she left."

"Weird how?"

"She brought Poppy to my room and asked us to stay inside because she was going to do some gardening and didn't want Poppy outside in case she cast some spells."

Drew frowned. "Gardening?" Because they'd just moved into the farmhouse, they hadn't had time to get the planter boxes installed that Noel wanted. That was the next project he'd planned to tackle after the chicken coop. "Doing what?"

Daisy shrugged. "She didn't say, but why would she be gardening when it was starting to get dark? And why would she be using spells?"

"Her air magic comes in handy. Maybe she wanted to rip something out," Drew guessed. "She hates that thorny holly bush near the water spigot. She's threatened to rip it out a few times."

"I don't know, Dad." Daisy looked up at him, worry in her young face. "She just seemed off. I can't explain it."

Drew pulled Daisy in for one more hug and said, "Don't worry. I'm sure she's fine." But as soon as he said the words, dread settled in his gut, and he knew right then something was seriously wrong.

"Buffy's dressed and ready for her walk," Poppy said as she bounded into the room with the small dog in her arms. Buffy was wearing a black sweater with little pink hearts all over it, and she had a bow in her hair.

Drew couldn't help but smile at Poppy. The way she doted on the shih tzu was really sweet. But his smile quickly faded as he clipped on Buffy's leash and told his girls, "I'm going to take Buffy out and then we'll figure out what to do about dinner. I'm sure your mom is going to be hungry when she turns up."

His forced optimism didn't seem to move Daisy, but Poppy glanced at the kitchen counter and then back at Drew and asked, "Can we have cookies while we wait?"

"Sure, pumpkin," Drew said absently.

"Thanks, Daddy." She ran to the jar and pulled out two cookies.

Daisy gave her father a flat stare. "You know you've been had, right? Mom already let her have some."

Drew ruffled Daisy's hair and said, "It's fine. And you don't need to tattle on your sister all the time. Siblings should have each other's backs," he said with a wink.

"You're going to change your mind when she's bouncing off the walls in ten minutes." Daisy walked out of the kitchen, shaking her head, and Drew had to admit that she likely had a point. But so did he.

The sound of the television blared from the other room and with Buffy's leash in hand, he stepped outside. A shiver of dread washed over him, and in that moment, nothing mattered except finding his wife. "Come on, Buffy. Help me find Noel."

The air was still and silent. There weren't any critters chirping or the rustling sounds of wildlife. Just nothingness, and it unnerved him. Buffy stuck to his side, forgoing her usual sniffing around as she kept her ears back on high alert.

"What is it, Buffy?" Drew asked her. But the dog just pressed in closer to him, and he took it as a sign that she didn't know what was making them both uneasy either.

After checking the holly tree and finding that it hadn't, in fact, been ripped out of the ground, Drew did a cursory glance at the rest of the vegetation and decided that Noel hadn't done any gardening. At least not outside. It was possible she'd been getting some starts ready in the barn for the spring garden, though they hadn't purchased any seeds yet, and he didn't know why she'd need spells for that.

When he pulled the barn door open, Buffy stopped in her tracks. Drew glanced down at her. "What is it?"

She glanced up at him and then back at the darkened barn. Then she jumped up, putting her front paws on his leg. He reached down and picked her up, letting her snuggle into his chest. After stuffing the leash in his pocket, he placed his hand on the stun gun that he carried for work that was still strapped to his belt and cautiously peered into the building.

He scanned carefully, peering through the darkness. Nothing appeared to be out of place. But the space beckoned to him, telling him that something had happened there. He reached in and flipped the switch on the wall, flooding the barn with light. The temperature dropped a good twenty degrees the moment he stepped into the building.

Standing completely still, he studied the entire barn, looking for anything out of place.

Nothing.

Everything was exactly as it was supposed to be.

Frustrated, knowing that he never went wrong when he trusted his gut, he moved toward the loft and climbed the ladder, dreading what he might find.

But there was nothing except a half-empty bag of grass seed up there.

"Noel," he said quietly, "what in the world went on here tonight?" When he looked down at the floor to the right of the barn door, he spotted the light reflecting off something silver.

With Buffy still plastered to his side, he scrambled down the ladder and over to the door. One glance at the shimmering device gave him his first clue.

It was Noel's phone.

She'd definitely been in the barn earlier. He reached down for the phone, and when he turned it over, he let out a growl of frustration. The screen was cracked, and the phone appeared to be dead. There was no telling what had gone on earlier that evening, but the one thing he knew for sure was that his wife would never leave her kids without a word and no way to contact her. Wherever she was, something was seriously wrong. He had to go out and look for her. Waiting wasn't an option.

Drew glanced down at the dog, who looked up at him with big, worried eyes. "Looks like it's going to be a long night, Buff. We'd better call in reinforcements."

CHAPTER 7

I'm going to kill him, Noel screamed at Clara. Once Clara had taken control of Noel's body, she'd sped off in Noel's car and had come straight to Woodlines. Now they were in the stockroom with Henry, the manager of the restaurant. The one who'd been calling her nonstop for days regarding Drew's birthday party.

The spirit who had taken over Noel's body laughed. "Henry, my dear, Noel isn't too pleased with you. I guess she didn't like that you shared your magic with me so that I could come back to you."

You guess? Noel raged at her. *You two stole my body. Took me away from my husband and kids!* Noel was so angry she thought she could rip them both apart with her bare hands if that were even a remote possibility.

"That's not news," the manager of Woodlines said. "I've been dealing with her terrible attitude for weeks now. But don't worry, darling. After we're done with our mission tonight, you won't be subjected to her for much longer. Once we get what we need, we can expel her altogether, just like I did to the poor soul who used to occupy this body five years ago."

Mission? What mission? And how exactly are they planning to expel me? Noel thought. Had she heard him right? He'd done this to someone else? What had happened to him? Was his poor soul haunting the place where they'd left him? *Oh gods. Does that mean if they expel me somewhere other than the farmhouse that I can't even watch my girls grow up?*

The urge to strangle Clara and Henry was enough to drive Noel mad. She desperately wanted to beat at the walls of whatever prison she'd been regulated to. But she didn't have control of her limbs, her will, or even her power. There was nothing to do other than yell into the darkness that was Clara's sticky consciousness. *You can't expel me from my own body*, Noel said as pure rage took over every molecule of her pathetic existence. Not when she wasn't willing to go, anyway.

"Oh, you'll want to go," Clara said, her tone light and airy as if she didn't have a care in the world. "Trust me on that one."

Henry slipped his arm around Clara and pulled her

in close, clutching her to his thin but muscular body. "I can't believe we finally did it, my love. After a hundred years apart, I finally get to hold you again."

Noel was so sick she wanted to vomit.

Clara pulled away from Henry and pressed her hand to her abdomen as bile rose up from the back of her throat.

"Darling? What's wrong?" Henry asked, brushing a lock of hair out of her eyes.

"I think I'm going to be sick." Clara bolted around him and retched right there in the stockroom.

"Clara, control yourself," Henry ordered her, his tone full of disapproval. "I told you if you didn't lock that soul away we'd have problems."

Clara turned to look at him. Tension filled her body, and Noel thought she might strike him. Instead, Clara glared at him and, with venom in her voice, said, "Don't you dare talk to me like that, Henry Thurston III. It's not the early 1900s anymore. Women have rights now. You'd do well to remember that. Treat me with respect or—"

"Or what, Clara?" His voice was dangerously low as he stepped in closer, cornering Clara. "May I remind you that the only reason you're here now is because I rescued you from that tiny little brothel in Storyville? I don't care what century it is. I own you and always will. You are magically bound to me. Or did you forget?"

"Or nothing," she said, lowering her gaze to the floor as a trickle of her fear ran through Noel's body.

"That's my girl," Henry said, pressing his palm to her cheek and caressing gently as if he hadn't just treated her like human garbage.

He's dangerous, Noel said, wondering if Henry could hear her, too. If they were connected, he might be able to.

He can't, Clara said in her mind.

You can hear not just what I say, but my thoughts, too? Noel gasped out. She didn't know why she was surprised. She shouldn't have been. They were sharing the same mind, body, and soul.

Of course I can, Clara said with a mental sigh. *It's exhausting if you must know the truth.*

I hope you aren't looking for an apology, Noel shot back. *You are the one who invaded me after all.*

Clara ignored her and went to clean up the vomit while Henry fumed about the smell.

You'll be miserable being attached to him for eternity, Noel said, trying anything to stop whatever they planned to do to expel her from her body.

It'll be better than haunting the farmhouse of the most boring, domestic people I've ever seen.

I don't believe you, Noel said mildly, knowing she was getting under Clara's skin.

He's not usually like that. Clara finished cleaning up and replaced the mop and the cleaning supplies. Just as she was turning around, Henry appeared and then inspected the mop. At first Noel thought he was just going to use it, but then he moved it about a half inch to the left in the supply cabinet. Then he turned his attention to the cleaning supplies. After an intense scrutiny, he twisted a bottle that Clara hadn't even used so that it was perfectly in line with the rest of the bottles.

"Did you see that, Clara?" Henry asked with one judgmental eyebrow raised. "That's how to put things away. Understand?"

"Yes," she said, sounding obedient. But Noel felt her rage like it was her own. Clara very much didn't like Henry's controlling ways.

You should do something about him, Noel whispered to Clara.

Shut up, she snapped as they both watched Henry disappear into the front of the restaurant.

I doubt that's going to happen, Noel mused. *I don't have anything else to do.*

Clara let out a huff of frustration before pulling a cigarette out of her skirt pocket and heading out the back door. As she lit it, Noel cried, *No!*

Clara ignored her and took a long drag that immediately resulted in a horrific coughing fit. It was the kind that made one's eyes water and feel as if they were drowning.

"Have you never smoked before?" Clara wheezed, pounding on her chest.

No. I actually care about my body, Noel said dryly.

"That was your choice, but not anymore," Clara said, rolling the cigarette back and forth between her thumb and forefinger. "I've been waiting a very long time for this. Stop yapping and let me enjoy it."

Noel was about to protest again, but she was overwhelmed by the intake of smoke and had to retreat into the corner of her mind to escape it. Once there, all she could do was think about her girls and Drew and pray that her husband found a way to figure out what had happened to her.

CHAPTER 8

After dropping the girls and Buffy off at Grandpa Lin's house, Drew got back into his truck and sent a group text to all four of Noel's sisters, asking if they'd seen her.

The replies rolled in one after another. None of them had seen her that day and they wanted to know what was going on. Drew wasn't sure what to say. He didn't want to lie, but he didn't want to cause a panic either. It was possible Noel had taken off to deal with something at the inn. He'd tried to call, but he'd only gotten the voice mail, which meant they were either busy or very slow. It was those nights when they let the service get their calls and they called back during business hours.

Instead of leaving a message, he decided to head to

town and just go there first. He texted the Townsend sisters to let them know that Noel was out, but her phone was broken and he was just trying to track her down. Then he asked them to please have her call him if they heard from her. That seemed to appease everyone except Abby.

Just as Drew was headed down the main highway, his phone rang. He picked it up through his Bluetooth. "Yes, Abby? Have you heard from Noel?"

"No, and your message freaked me out. Something's not right, Drew. I can feel it all the way down to my toes. Now, what's really going on?"

At least now he had confirmation that he wasn't crazy about his insistence that something was off. If Abby felt it too, then it wasn't just him being paranoid. "Before I got home from work, Noel left the house without telling the girls where she was going. I also found her phone broken in the barn. That's all I know."

"She just left without letting the girls know?" Abby gasped out. "She wouldn't do that!"

"I agree. That's why I'm headed to town to look for her," Drew said, turning down Main Street.

"Do you want me to meet you there?" Abby asked.

Drew knew she wanted him to say yes. Abby was a doer, much like all the Townsend sisters. Sitting around and waiting for news wasn't their MO. But still… He shook his head even though she couldn't see him. "No.

On the off chance there is trouble, I don't want my kids' favorite aunt to end up in the middle of it."

She was silent for a long moment.

"That doesn't mean there's trouble," Drew said, trying to reassure her, but there was no denying the dread that curled in his stomach.

"You don't believe that and neither do I," Abby said, seeing right through his feeble attempt to keep her calm.

"No, I guess I don't," Drew admitted. "But I don't want to worry about you while I'm out here looking for Noel. We both know this is wildly out of character for her, and if I do happen to find her, we have no idea what we'd be stepping into." Drew didn't want to sound dramatic, but in his profession, not much surprised him anymore. He'd seen too much in his time on the job.

"You won't have to worry about me," Abby insisted. "All I'm going to do is look around. You can't stop me, Drew."

"No, I guess I can't," Drew said, both anxious and relieved that he'd have someone else looking for Noel. "Just… be careful."

"I will, and I'll call if I see anything at all."

The call ended, and Drew realized that somehow while he'd been talking to Abby, the truck had seemed to steer itself to the inn, and he was just about to park in the empty spot reserved for Noel. He cursed under his breath after realizing that his wife's vehicle was nowhere to be seen. That meant it was highly unlikely she was there. He still had to check, though.

The light to the right of the front door was out, and Drew made a mental note to change the bulb. But when he went to reach for the doorknob, his foot came down on an uneven surface and made a sickening crunching sound.

He quickly stepped back and peered down at the porch, only to realize that the bulb wasn't just out. The entire sconce had been ripped off the wall of the inn and was lying shattered right in front of the door.

Drew sprang into action. He grabbed his Taser in one hand while he turned the doorknob and then unceremoniously threw it open.

He heard a startled cry that sounded a lot like Bianca. Hiding his Taser behind his back, Drew stepped into the inn, taking his time to look for threats. When he didn't see any, he secured his Taser and then walked over to the front desk where Bianca was shaking like a leaf. "Hey, I'm sorry," Drew said. "I didn't mean to scare you."

"Drew," she said with a huge sigh. "Thank goodness it's you. I..." She shook her head and flopped down into the wooden chair and leaned forward, trying to suck in air as if she were having a panic attack.

"Bianca!" He slipped behind the counter and

crouched beside her as he rubbed her back with one hand, trying to soothe her. "You're okay. Whatever happened, you're okay now."

Tears slipped down her ghostly pale face. "I'm not okay. Noel f-f-fired me."

"Noel was here?" he asked, his heart racing. "Just before I got here?"

Bianca nodded as the tears consumed her.

"But why?"

Holding up one arm, Bianca pointed toward the back room that was just behind the counter.

Drew stared through the open door, and when he caught a glimpse of the safe door that was open, he stood abruptly and headed for the safe only to find that it was completely empty. His heart sank all the way to the floor.

The safe was empty.

The emergency cash she'd always kept there was gone.

Why? The word kept flashing over and over again in his mind.

Drew walked back over to Bianca. "Did she say anything?"

"No," Bianca said, wiping her tears. "The guy who was with her did all the talking."

"What guy?" Had someone taken Noel against her will? It was the only logical explanation at that point.

"I don't know. He looked sort of familiar, but he had a fedora hat on that was covering his eyes, and I'm just not sure. I'm sorry, Drew. I'm just in shock. I don't really know what happened."

He nodded and quickly headed for the computer that was thankfully still on the desk. After a few taps on the keys, he found what he wanted and hit Play on the evening's security footage.

Four different perspectives flashed on the computer screen. One for the front porch, one for the back door, a third for the kitchen door, and the fourth for the front desk. There was nothing at first, and Drew sped up the playback and paused it the moment someone appeared at the front entrance.

Right there on the screen was his wife, holding hands with a tall man whose frame was indeed familiar. They paused just in front of the door long enough for the man to pull Noel into his arms, bend her back, and then kiss her for all he was worth. Her arms were around his neck, holding on tightly, and when he pulled up, she was smiling up at him.

Drew hit Pause and then printed out the picture. After snatching the paper from the printer tray underneath the check-in counter, he pocketed it and then forced himself to watch the rest of the video. After Noel and the man entered the front door, he turned his attention to the camera at the front desk. Bianca appeared, a surprised look on her face, but it shortly turned to one of confusion and then horror as she watched Noel and the man hold hands while they went back and raided the safe.

The audio was off, but when Noel and the man returned, it looked like Bianca asked what was going on. That's when the man grabbed her and pushed her up against the wall. He didn't hit her, but he said something in her ear that Noel seemed to repeat. As Noel and the man left, Bianca slid down the wall and broke down in tears.

Drew closed his eyes and counted to ten, trying to compartmentalize his feelings. He was both deeply angry and confused. But at that moment, he needed to reassure Bianca. He turned around and spotted her wiping her eyes with a tissue. "I'm so sorry about tonight, Bianca," he said. "I wish I knew what else to say, but I just don't have anything other than that right now."

She nodded, worry in her kind eyes. "I'm sorry, too. I know this can't be easy for you either."

"No, it isn't," he admitted. "But I'll deal with it. I don't know why Noel tried to fire you, but I think it's safe to say she isn't in her right mind. If it's not too much to ask, do you think you could stay on at least until I figure out what's going on? If you don't want to, I understand, but—"

"I'll do it," she said, standing taller and looking more determined. "I love this job. I don't want to leave and…" She shook her head. "I agree that Noel was not herself."

"Thank you," Drew said, already moving toward the front door. "You have no idea how much I appreciate this."

"You don't need to thank me," Bianca said quietly. "I've been in your shoes once before. No one deserves that."

Drew nodded once and then left. On the way home, he picked up his daughters from Lincoln's house.

"Did you find Noel?" Lincoln asked immediately when he opened the door to his son-in-law.

Drew nodded. "Yes, she had to take care of some business at the inn. Everything is fine. She's safe and sound." But was she really? Drew had no idea. His wife was acting completely out of character, and he had no idea how to deal with it. For tonight, he just needed to get his girls and go home to be alone with his thoughts. Filling her dad in on the drama wasn't something he was prepared to do. Not yet anyway.

"Oh, good. I'll stop worrying," Lin said with a smile. "Tell her to call me tomorrow when she has a chance."

Drew nodded and tried to tamp down the guilt that clawed at his throat. He had no idea if he'd even see Noel tomorrow. But he had to take it one step at a time. "Will do. Thanks again for watching the girls."

"Anytime."

As Drew walked his girls to the truck, Daisy looked up at him. "Where's Mom?"

"The inn." He needed to tell them something, and considering he was still in the dark himself, the lie would have to do. "There was a staffing emergency, so she'll likely stay over tonight."

"Oh. Okay." Daisy still looked a little troubled but appeared to accept his explanation.

"Will she be home tomorrow?" Poppy asked with a big yawn.

"I hope so, baby," he said and buckled her into the truck.

"Good." She leaned her head back and closed her eyes. In seconds she was asleep.

Once they were home, both girls went straight to bed.

Drew went to the rarely used liquor cabinet, poured himself two fingers of whiskey, and sat in the living room, staring at the printout of his wife kissing another man and trying to remember what life was like before everything had come crashing down around him.

CHAPTER 9

"We're not going to get far on this," Henry complained from the driver's seat of Noel's SUV. They were parked on the side of the road at a pull out on the main highway while Henry decided what he wanted to do next.

Noel hated the man with a passion. If thoughts could kill, he'd have been dead the minute he'd forced Clara to go in and steal all the money out of Noel's safe. The money she'd worked so hard for when it had just been her and Daisy before Drew had walked back into her life. She'd known him growing up of course, but they'd both gone their own way until they'd found each other as adults. Then they'd built a beautiful family and life together.

Henry was the one trying to steal it all, and it was

clear to Noel that Clara was just a pawn in his sick game. He planned to rob the inn and a number of the Keating Hollow businesses so that they could run off together on their sick Bonnie and Clyde adventure. Or he *had* until Noel had gotten Clara to mention that none of the businesses kept cash on hand anymore. There wasn't anything to take since they dropped their deposits at the banks each night.

She was surprised he hadn't realized that since he'd been running Woodlines, but she supposed a man who was from the early 1900s probably had his quirks.

"We need a place where we can steal products to sell," Henry was musing.

Noel immediately thought of Enchanted Jewelers. It was just a few doors down from the sheriff's station.

"The jewelry store," Clara said. "I know where it is."

"Excellent thinking, Clara darling. Diamonds are always a good plan." He put the SUV into gear and headed that direction.

Noel mentally berated herself for thinking it. If she hadn't, they wouldn't be headed for a smash-and-grab before they fled town. Away from her kids. Away from Drew. Her soul ached as despair hit her hard.

Stop being so depressing, Clara said. *It'll be easier for you if you'll just accept your fate. You might even enjoy yourself a little. If there's one thing I can say about Henry, it's that he'd never boring. I never have been either.*

Is that what you keep telling yourself? Noel asked her. *That being abused is exciting?*

It's better than being trapped on this earth, destined to walk alone, Clara said in her mind. Then she showed Noel an image of herself haunting that old farmhouse for an entire century before Henry came for her and promised her a life of adventure where she'd never be alone again.

It was easy to see why she thought this was better than her previous ghostly existence. But Noel knew that eventually she'd regret it. Henry had an evil streak that would destroy Clara sooner rather than later.

Even that's better than what I've endured, Clara mentally told Noel.

I'm sorry to hear you think that, Noel answered. *If you'd given me and my family a real chance, I think you'd have found that we could have helped you. You didn't need to turn to this.*

You don't know what you're talking about, Clara denied.

Maybe she didn't, but Noel knew mediums and would have been happy to consult with them if asked.

Shut up, Clara ordered her.

I wasn't even talking, Noel said. *Sorry I can't turn my brain off. You'll just have to deal with it.*

Clara let out an irritated huff and then ignored Noel for the rest of the drive to the jewelry store.

Henry didn't even bother trying to park where the

car wouldn't be seen. Noel knew that security cameras would see it and as soon as Drew looked at it, he'd think she was a part of the heist. Pure rage made her see red, but then another thought occurred to her. If Drew saw it, he'd come for her. Maybe, just maybe, if she was able to see him, she could find a way to communicate what had happened.

Clara let out an amused snort. *You wish.*

Henry jumped out of the SUV and then waved for Clara to follow. It took Henry less than thirty seconds to magic his way into the store. Noel had to admit it; the man did have some powerful magic. That wasn't good news for her. Once they were out of Keating Hollow, if he was serious about expelling her from her own body, she was starting to believe that he could probably do it. Her only hope was to make sure she didn't leave town.

I'm taking this body out of this town, Clara said. *Get used to it.*

Noel didn't answer her. Instead, she started issuing rapid-fire orders. *Get the tennis bracelet. No, not that one. The emerald one. And the sapphires, too. You'll want a wedding ring. One nicer than mine. Something with lots of carats. One for each finger.*

On and on, Noel pointed out one jewelry piece after another, trying to keep them in the store as long as possible. Clara was loaded down with diamonds, and then suddenly something miraculous happened. Noel could feel her limbs. Her movement was coming back to her. She was partially in control, but not fully. Clara would try to move toward the cases of jewels, while Noel tried to run for the door. The net effect was them running into one of the display cases. Noel let out a grunt and then a cry when she was backhanded by Henry.

"I told you to stuff the pieces in a bag, not wear every damned thing in the place! Diamonds absorb magic, you fool. If you keep it up, you're going to lose your control over her."

Noel's eyes widened. That was the reason she could feel her body again? She nodded once and then scrambled away, desperate to hit the panic button and get as many diamonds on her body as possible.

But Henry was keeping a close eye on her, ordering her to fill his messenger bag with item after item. Never letting her more than six inches from him.

He's going to kill you if you try anything, Clara said, seemingly comfortable with her retreat into Noel's mind as she let her deal with Henry.

He can try, but he won't succeed, Noel shot back. Not now that she had her will and mobility back. She could feel her power returning as well, and now that she knew what to expect, she wasn't letting them take her again.

"Pay attention!" Henry ordered and then shoved her from the back, sending her right into a display case.

Noel scrambled back to her feet and was just completely done with Henry. Her magic swirled to her fingertips and just as she was about to let it fly, Clara said, *I wouldn't.*

Too late. Noel aimed for the large chandelier hanging just above them. The moment it hit, she scrambled to the side and barely missed being crushed.

Henry went down, cursing her the entire time.

Noel ran for the case nearest a register in the back. Henry was ordering her to come help him, but she ignored him. She was on a mission now, and there was no turning back. Just as she reached the counter and was sliding her fingers over the panic button, a blast of magic hit her square in the back, and she crumbled to her knees, barely able to breathe. Her heart was beating so fast she was certain it would pound right out of her chest.

"You think you're clever, Noel?" Henry asked as he peered down at her, his pupils pure black. "You can't win in a match up against me," he snarled as blood trickled down his temple from where the chandelier had hit him. "Your air magic has nothing on my spirit powers."

That explained why he could merge spirits with living people.

"Maybe," she said calmly, "but I bet even spirit witches have problems healing from bullet wounds."

Henry spun, magic swirling around him in brilliant red and orange light. But as soon as he lunged for the deputy behind him, Adrian Hunt pulled the trigger, and Henry crumpled to the ground.

Noel let out a cry of relief and felt her control over her body start to wane. Her feet were tingling, and she was having trouble focusing.

Henry used his magic to strip you of a lot of the diamonds, Clara said. *You didn't notice?*

Noel hadn't. She'd been too busy trying to survive.

Deputy Sheriff Adrian Hunt walked over to Noel and frowned down at her. "Noel? What's going on?"

Noel used the last of her strength to lift her hands and said, "I tried to rob this store. Arrest me."

"Why don't we wait until Sheriff Baker gets here?" he suggested.

"No!" Noel ordered. "Handcuff me, or Clara might take over." Noel held his gaze and said, "Do it. Now."

The last thing Noel remembered was the cold steel of the metal cuffs chaffing against her wrists.

CHAPTER 10

Drew sat in his chair, an untouched whiskey in his hand while he battled his dark thoughts. They were all over the place, contemplating everything from marriage counseling to custody battles. Was it really just three nights ago when he'd been at the beach with Noel, the two of them seemingly more in love than ever? And now here he was, in the middle of the night, wondering how he could have been so blind.

Willful ignorance.

Wasn't it that same night when Noel kept getting all those phone calls and she'd said it was the inn? Now he was certain she'd lied. In all their years together, even before she'd hired a manager, there'd rarely been nights where anyone called at all. Keating Hollow Inn just wasn't that busy, and when it was, Noel usually had it covered.

Now that he thought back, Noel had been distracted for at least a couple of weeks. She'd been secretive on her phone, quickly turning it off when he'd walk into the room or turning it face down so he wouldn't see an incoming text.

Each incident on its own hadn't been an issue, but taken all together, he wondered how he'd been such a fool.

His phone gave a loud trill, shaking him out of his grim reality. He glanced down at it and sat up straighter when he spotted Deputy Sheriff Hunt's name.

"Baker here. What's the problem?" Drew asked.

"Uh, Sheriff," Hunt said, sounding nervous. "We have a situation. You're going to need to come to the station."

Drew got to his feet and took his still-full drink to the kitchen. "Lay it on me."

"There's been a robbery at Enchanted Jewelry. We've made one arrest. Our other suspect is being seen by a healer after suffering a gunshot wound to the shoulder, and he will be processed as soon as Healer Whipple gives us clearance."

"You shot a suspect in a robbery?" Drew asked. "Was he armed?"

"Yes, sir. With magic."

WISDOM OF THE WITCH

"I see. It sounds like you have everything under control," he said. "Are you sure you don't want to handle it from here?"

"Sir, the suspect we arrested is your wife."

Drew froze. "What did you just say?"

Hunt cleared his throat and stammered before forcing out, "Your wife Noel was caught red-handed with enough diamonds on her person to rank the crime a Class 1 felony. I can take the lead on this, but—"

"I'll be right there." Drew ended the call and turned around, intending to grab his keys and go. But when he found Poppy standing in the doorway, holding the picture he'd printed of Noel and her lover, his heart sank. How had he been so careless as to leave that out where she might find it? "Poppy," he said, gently taking the photo from her. "This is—" He didn't know how to finish that sentence. There was no sugar-coating the obvious. Her mother was embracing another man. How did one explain that to their six-year-old? "That's—"

"Why is the ghost at Mommy's inn?" Poppy asked.

"Huh?" Drew moved to crouch down in front of her.

"Is that where Mommy sent her?"

"Uh, Poppy, what do you mean? Do you see the ghost in that picture?" he asked.

"Yes," Poppy said impatiently. "She's right here." She pointed to Noel.

Drew studied her, not sure what to make of his

daughter's declaration. Then he decided he just had to ask her straight out. "You don't think that woman looks like Mommy?"

Poppy scrunched up her face. "No. Why would you say that? This is the ghost from the loft. The one who made me pour the seed on your head. She's the reason I got in trouble and couldn't go to my friend's party."

A chill slithered over Drew's skin, and he recognized that his daughter was telling the truth. She had been all along. "Tell me about the day in the loft. How did the ghost make you dump the seed?" Daisy had said she'd watched Poppy do it. He'd believed his eldest daughter. But now he was certain he hadn't gotten the entire story.

"She just appeared and told me to pour the seed on you. I told her you wouldn't like it, but she got mad and then forced me to do it."

"You mean she moved your arms and made you do it?" Drew asked, trying to understand.

"Sort of." Her eyes turned glassy with tears when she added, "I felt like she was inside me, making me do it."

Possession? The spirit had possessed his daughter? His voice was shaking when he asked, "Then what happened?"

"You yelled and she left." Poppy shuddered with the memory.

Drew's entire body was tense, ready for a fight with the spirit. "Have you felt the ghost since then, Poppy?"

She shook her head. "I think it's because she's in the barn and I'm in here."

"Who's in the barn? The ghost?" he asked.

"Yes." Poppy looked down at her feet. "I told Mommy I couldn't go out there. She said she'd take care of it."

Fear consumed every inch of Drew's heart. Noel's phone had been in the barn. She'd been in there. She'd told Daisy she was going to garden, yet there were zero signs of that. She'd been in the barn when her phone had been shattered, and then she'd left everyone behind and was seen kissing another man. Now she was in jail for felony theft.

All of those things were so out of character for Noel. He suddenly felt ashamed for believing that she'd cheat on him.

Drew hugged his daughter tightly and said, "Thank you for telling me, sweetheart. You don't need to worry about that ghost. Mommy and Daddy are making sure she leaves us alone for good."

She pulled back and gave him a tired smile. "Good. Can I have some water now?"

Drew got her a drink and then tucked her into bed with Daisy and told them he was off to the station. On the way, he called Lincoln and asked if he could stay with the girls.

"There's something you're not telling me," Lincoln said.

"It's Noel," Drew said, acknowledging that Lincoln had a right to know what was going on with his daughter. "I'm about 99% certain she's been possessed by a ghost that was occupying our farmhouse. She's done some seriously out of character things today and is now in jail for robbing the jewelry store. I'm calling in reinforcement from the pros and hopefully by morning, we'll have her back home, safe, sound, and ghost-free."

Silence.

"Lincoln?" Drew asked. "You there?"

"Yeah. That was... a lot," Lincoln said. "Possessed?"

"Possessed," Drew confirmed. "But don't worry. She won't be for long."

"Maybe I should come down to the station," Lincoln said, and Drew could hear him moving around as if he were getting ready to do just that.

"I really would rather you go keep an eye on the girls. I know Daisy is responsible enough to watch her sister, but after everything that's happened today, I'd feel better if they had someone they can count on right there in the house."

"Yeah, okay. I'll head over right now."

"Thank you, Lincoln. I appreciate it."

"No need to thank me, Drew. I love those girls. You know that."

"Yes, I do. I'll call you with an update when there's something to report."

"I appreciate it."

Drew ended the call and sped so fast to the station that he made it there in under five minutes. A record.

He strode in past the night clerk and right into Hunt's office. "Where is she?"

"Cell two, by herself. I'm sorry, man," Hunt said, getting to his feet to greet Drew. "I wasn't going to arrest her until I spoke to you, but she insisted. Made me promise to cuff her there on the spot."

Drew clapped him on the shoulder. "Good job, man. You did exactly the right thing."

"I'm still not sure about that, but I'll take it," Hunt said.

"You should." Drew strode down the hall and into the secured area. Just before he got to cell two, he paused and took a fortifying breath. Then he went in.

His wife was sitting on the bare bed, staring straight ahead. "Noel?" When she didn't respond, he asked, "Or is it Clara?"

The person who occupied his wife's body turned to glare at him with an icy chill. "How is it I spent a hundred years in one prison and now I'm right back in another?"

Ah, definitely Clara. "You probably shouldn't have stolen someone else's body and then robbed a jewelry store," he said.

"Ha. Like I had a choice." She turned to stare at the wall.

Drew called out, "Hunt?"

His deputy was there in seconds. "Yes, boss?"

"I need you to call Cash Moses and Harlow Thane. Their number is in the contacts database. Tell them my wife has been possessed."

"Uh, boss?"

Drew met Hunt's eyes. "Yes?"

"Are you sure? She seemed a little out of control earlier, but she definitely seemed like Noel."

Drew opened his mouth to answer but then paused as Noel got up and walked very slowly over to the cell bars.

Hunt watched her carefully until she suddenly reached through the bars and tried to grab for his throat. He jumped back, protecting his chest with both arms. "What the hell?"

"Thought you'd like to know what it's going to be like once you expel me from this body."

"So... possessed then?" Hunt asked Drew.

"Possessed."

CHAPTER 11

"You're gonna pay extra for this one, Sheriff," Harlow Thane said to Drew as she strode into the cell block.

"Definitely," Cash Moses said, stifling a yawn. "You do realize it's almost three in the morning, right?"

"Charge whatever you want. Just bill me personally," Drew said, getting to his feet to greet the couple. After Clara had tried to scratch his eyes out, he'd opted to wait for them on the other side of the bars.

"You personally?" Harlow scanned Noel's body with a critical eye. "Noel?"

"It's Clara," she said, infuriating Noel one more time. Ever since she'd woken up in jail, she'd been regulated back into the recesses of her own mind. Clara had been berating her for hours, claiming she'd ruined her life. Replacing one prison for another one. And the entire time, Noel had done her best to ignore her.

There was no use fueling her delusions. She knew Drew wouldn't rest until she was freed from her prison.

Cash looked over at Harlow. "Are you ready to kick some spirit butt?"

"Butt? That seems mild for the situation." Harlow let out a bark of laughter while she pulled out what looked like some sort of metal spike.

"I'm working on my potty mouth," Cash said as he lined up a row of candles in front of where he and Harlow were standing. Over the past month, ever since Harlow had dealt with her own ghost possession, Harlow and Cash had opened up their spirit hunting business to those who were in need. They'd gone from being celebrity ghost hunters to taking only cases that helped people. Noel was grateful for both of them and vowed to make something special for them when this was all over.

"Noel? Are you doing okay?" Harlow called conversationally.

Noel tried to nod and then realized why it wasn't working. *Tell them I'm here and ready,* she ordered Clara.

"No." Clara crossed her arms over her chest and glared at everyone.

Harlow laughed. "Nice try, but it's not gonna work with me. I've battled and beaten way worse than you, babe." She turned to Cash. "Ready?"

Cash nodded. "Let's do this."

Together they started chanting an incantation that sounded like another language. Probably Latin, but Noel couldn't place it. Almost immediately her fingers and toes started to tingle, signaling that Clara was losing her grip on Noel's body.

The pair chanted louder and louder and louder, slowly but surely breaking the connection that Clara had on Noel.

Clara's fear rolled through Noel, and Noel started seeing flashes of injustices that Clara had been subjected to over the course of her life. Poverty, neglectful parents, and her time at Storyville, which had never been her choice at all. Her mother had sold her off to the brothel owner to pay a debt.

Then finally the handsome and powerful Henry had come along and rescued her, only to put her back in a cage where he'd forced her to live his life of crime for a few years before she died in a car chase.

It was then that Clara had looked to the sky, ready to be free of the chains of this world, but Henry had cursed her to roam the earth, vowing to find a way that they could be together again. That was when she'd been trapped at Noel's current farmhouse for nearly a hundred years.

All I ever wanted was to be free, Clara said.

Cash and Harlow were closing in. Harlow had her iron stake in her right hand, no doubt ready to attack the spirit the minute she was separated from Noel's body. And Cash had an iron chain in case he needed to trap the spirit when it broke free.

I'm being sucked back into nothing, Clara said, her voice cracking. Her pain nearly paralyzed Noel, and all she felt for the woman was sadness. She'd never had anything to be grateful for on this earth.

"Wait!" Noel cried, finally able to speak aloud. "Wait one minute!" She turned to catch her husband's eye. "Tell them to send her to the sky, not wherever they're sending her now. She wants to be free."

The two mediums stopped chanting and peered at Noel.

Noel turned her attention back to the mediums. "Can you do that? Send her to the sky?"

"Not exactly," Harlow said. "We can release her, but it's up to her to go on her own. If she doesn't, she could potentially cause even more havoc. It's been my experience that spirits who have been around this long generally have no interest in leaving."

Noel shook her head. "Not this time. She's never

had the choice before. Please, just give her the opportunity?"

"Are you sure? Depending on her power, she could latch onto you again, and I can't guarantee we can do this again so soon," Harlow said. "The energy it takes is a lot."

"I understand," Noel said. "I just… She wants to go. I can feel it deep in my soul."

Harlow and Cash shared a glance, and then Harlow nodded. The two of them held hands as they chanted one last time. "Release now, spirit of the earth. Let go and find the light!"

Noel's skin tingled with heat as if she'd been blasted by the sun, and then Clara was gone. She watched as the spirit in question took up the same silvery shape she'd had back at the farmhouse. But there was no more taunting or terrorizing. She just floated there in the middle of the jail, staring up at the light that was shining down on her.

The spirit took one last glance at Noel, mouthed *Thank you*, and then floated up and into the light, plunging the rest of them in the jailhouse back into a bunker of gray.

"Well, what do you know?" Harlow said with a surprised laugh. "I thought for sure we'd be battling her again." She walked over to Noel and placed an arm around her waist, holding her up. "You did good, Noel.

Thank you. It's always a joy to send spirits to the light. Rare, but a joy."

"I just... She never had a choice," Noel repeated and then burst into tears as Drew gathered her into his arms and whispered over and over how much he loved her.

CHAPTER 12

*A*fter taking a few days to recover from her ordeal, Noel finally got out of the house and headed to the inn. She had a few things to check on, but mostly she wanted to talk to Bianca. There were some amends to make there. The money that Henry and Clara had taken out of the safe had been found in the glove compartment of her SUV and would soon be going right back where it belonged.

It was a sunny spring morning when Noel walked into the inn. The light was streaming through the front windows, and it looked just as peaceful and charming as ever. It was only when she saw Bianca flinch at the sight of her that Noel was reminded this wasn't just any normal visit.

Tears stung Noel's eyes as she walked over to the

desk, but she kept her distance from Bianca. She could tell she made the other woman nervous. Of course she did. Even though Drew had already told Bianca what had actually been going on that night, it was clear that her manager was still struggling in the aftermath.

"I'm so sorry, Bianca," Noel started, her voice cracking. "I hope you know I would never treat you the way—"

Bianca launched herself at Noel, hugging her so tightly Noel was having trouble breathing. But she wrapped her arms around her friend and held on tight.

"I knew something was seriously wrong," Bianca said between her tears. "That person who came in here was nothing like the woman I've come to love like a sister. I'm so glad you're back."

"Oh, thank the goddess. I was so worried that ghost had messed this up for both of us." Noel pulled back and gave Bianca a shaky smile. "I don't know what I'd do if I lost you. Not just as the manager of this place, but as my friend."

"You're not going to lose me," she said. "You know I love it here. I was just so worried about you and Drew and the girls."

"We're fine. Or at least the girls and I are fine. Drew is having trouble letting any of us out of his sight, but I suspect he'll get past it soon enough."

The two women held onto each other for a long

while as they got caught up on the business of running the inn, and when they were done, Noel said, "You are coming to Drew's birthday party on Sunday, right? We've moved it to my dad's."

"If we can find someone to man the desk, I wouldn't miss it," Bianca said.

"Already got that covered. The new maintenance guy said he'd handle it." Noel glanced up just in time to see the man in question walk in. He was tall, lean, and muscular with thick black curls and bright blue eyes. Striking was the only way to describe him.

"Mateo, hey," Noel said, reaching out to give him a quick hug. "Bianca, this is Mateo. He used to work here for a little while right after I purchased the inn, so he knows his way around. He'll be handling any and all maintenance and upgrades to the inn. He can also chip in when we need someone to fill in for a few hours."

Bianca blinked twice, looking thunderstruck.

"Mateo, this is Bianca. She's our inn manager. As I mentioned before, I mostly just oversee things and run events these days."

Mateo held his hand out to Bianca, who finally seemed to get ahold of herself as she did the same and said, "Nice to meet you."

"I look forward to working with you, Bianca." Then he gave her a mock tip of his hat and disappeared into the kitchen.

Bianca turned to Noel and said, "Tell me you hired him just for me."

Noel threw her head back and laughed. "He's all yours as long as he keeps the windows and roof from leaking."

"I bet he's a multitasker," she said in a seductive voice, making both women cackle.

∼

Noel's next visit wasn't nearly as rewarding. The small white cottage that sat in the middle of the redwoods looked rundown and like no one had lived there for ages. Not unlike the farmhouse that she and Drew had purchased before the renovations. She wasn't even sure if the owner was in, but she bit down on her bottom lip and knocked anyway.

A few moments later, a man she hardly recognized opened the door and gave her a very faint whisper of a smile. "Noel. This is a surprise." His voice was full of rasp, like he'd been a thirty-five-year smoker, though he couldn't have been more than forty himself. "Come in."

She stepped into the rustic, yet neat, cabin and looked around. There was a serviceable sectional that made up the entirety of the living room but zero pictures or art on the walls. It was void of both life and color. She glanced back at him, still reeling about how much he'd changed since Harlow and Cash had exorcised the spirit from his body.

As it turned out, the man who'd taken over Henry's identity five years ago was really named Gus Causey, and he'd been a notoriously powerful magic-wielding gangster back in his day. He'd told Clara that he'd expelled his host from his body, but he hadn't. He didn't contain that much power. According to Harlow, almost no spirits did. So Noel was never really in danger of completely losing her physical form, but if she hadn't found a way to fight back, she could have lost herself to Clara.

"How are you doing?" Noel asked him.

"As good as can be expected, I guess," he said, leaning against the counter and rubbing his shoulder. "Healer Whipple worked miracles on my shoulder. I didn't even need stitches. But it still aches, like a phantom pain. She said it would go away in a few weeks."

"That's good. Real good," Noel said, grateful he hadn't been hurt worse.

He pressed his lips together in a thin line and then said, "What can I do for you today?"

"It's not what you can do for me, really" she said, feeling anxious. "More like what we can do for each other."

He frowned. "I'm not sure I'm following."

She swallowed hard and studied the tall man's angular face. It was weird. His bone structure and physical appearance were exactly the same as when the spirit had been possessing him, but now that Gus was gone, there was zero trace of the arrogant restaurant manager, the domineering force who dared anyone to cross him. Instead, all she saw was a tired, easygoing man in his ripped jeans, white T-shirt, and flannel button-down.

Noel ran a hand through her hair, trying to calm her nerves. "I came by because I wanted to see if you'll have coffee with me next week. Well, with me and Imogen, Harlow's sister."

He raised his eyebrows, clearly confused. "I guess, but why?"

She let out a nervous laugh and then finally just said, "Listen, I know I'm coming across as a bit of a weirdo, but Harlow was telling me that after people are subjected to a possession, it can really affect them in ways that no one else can understand. Imogen was possessed once, and it nearly ruined her life. A lot longer than just one night like me. We decided to try a biweekly coffee meeting, just to talk, maybe share experiences... or not. Just be there for each other, and I wanted to see if you're interested."

"A recovering possession support group?" he asked, looking cynical.

"Yeah," she said with a small chuckle. "I guess it's exactly like that."

He chewed on the side of his cheek, and when he started to shake his head, Noel grabbed his hand and said, "I know it's still very fresh, and I don't want to pressure you. I just want you to know there are people here in Keating Hollow who care. I'm one of them."

Henry stared down at her for what seemed like an eternity and then finally nodded. "Okay, I'll try it. Give me the details and I'll try to make it."

Instantly, Noel felt a weight lifted off her shoulders, and she didn't quite know why. Maybe it was because he'd lived with a spirit taking over his entire life for so long, and not one person noticed. But Noel wasn't going to let that happen again. Not in Keating Hollow. Not in the town that she'd always thought looked after their own.

"Incantation Café. I'll text you the date and time," she said and then hesitated for just a second before she asked, "Do you think I could give you a hug?"

He let out a short huff of laughter. "I never thought you were much of a hugger."

"You know what? I wasn't, but it appears this week I am. So what do you say?"

Henry answered by holding his arms out, and Noel walked right into his embrace, careful not to jostle his injured shoulder, and then poured every ounce of friendship she could muster into the hug.

Henry's breathing turned shallow, and she heard an audible hitch just before she felt his silent sob. And she knew then that, no matter what happened in the future, she'd always find a way to be there for him. They were linked now. And even though the circumstances that had brought them there had been horrific, she felt in her soul that this man would be the bestie she'd never had before.

When they finally pulled apart, Henry wiped at his eyes and let out a shaky laugh. "I didn't mean to fall apart like that."

"But isn't that exactly what I came here for?" she asked, smiling softly. "To offer support?"

He gave her a wry smile. "Yeah, I guess so."

As he walked her to the door, he said, "Don't forget to thank that husband of yours. If it wasn't for him insisting that Harlow and Cash check to make sure I wasn't possessed anymore, I'm fairly certain I'd be sitting in a jail cell right now."

"I will. He's a good one, isn't he?"

"Maybe the best." He gave her one last hug before saying, "If he has a brother, send him my way."

Noel let out a cackle of laughter and said, "He doesn't, but never fear. We'll find you someone worthy. Just give me time."

CHAPTER 13

"Happy birthday, babe," Noel said, wrapping her arms around Drew. "I'm sorry it isn't the fancy catered bash I'd envisioned, but with Henry leaving, Woodlines just couldn't pull it off."

Drew gazed down into his gorgeous wife's face and said, "Didn't you know this is all I ever wanted anyway? Don't get me wrong, I appreciate the effort and would have loved the raw bar, but this"—he waved at the sea of people who'd shown up for their potluck barbeque at Lin's house—"is heaven on earth. Good burgers, good beer, good friends, and a gorgeous, loving family. What more does a guy need?"

Noel laughed. "When you put it that way, I guess not much, other than maybe a handyman to fix the chicken coop door that won't close all the way."

"Hey, woman, I already told you that's because of the warped door. It's not the builder's fault. A new one is on the way."

"That's right," Lincoln said, arriving with a fresh beer for the birthday boy. "Do not disparage the chicken coop masters."

Noel rolled her eyes. "Whatever you two say."

A horn beeped, and when Drew glanced up, he spotted a purple golf cart coming right for them. Wanda, the town Realtor and Abby's best friend, was driving and blasting Pharrell Williams's "Happy." The cart was full of the Townsend clan's children as they all waved their hands in the air and sang along. Wanda parked it near Abby's old studio and then designated one of the older children as the DJ before walking over to Noel and Drew.

"We definitely weren't going to get that if we'd had this party at Woodlines," Drew said, grinning at Wanda. "They look like they're having a blast."

"They weren't the only ones," Wanda said as she did a little dance. "There is just nothing more fun than taking those kids for a spin."

Noel raised her eyebrows at her. "Are you saying that's more fun than the golf cart races?"

"Oh, hmm, you've got me there. I'd say it's a toss-up then. Golf carts just bring the fun, no matter what."

Abby walked up and gave her friend a hug. After

that, everyone seemed to be talking at once. Everyone but Drew. He was just in the middle of it all, taking it in. This family that he'd married into was loud and overwhelming at times, but they were everything he'd ever wanted as a kid. His parents were great, but it had just been the three of them. Now he felt like he was related to at least half the town, and he loved every one of them.

It seemed as if it was more than one man could ever ask for.

"Hey, did you all hear that Woodlines is shutting down?" Wanda said loudly over the chatter.

"What?" Drew asked, already feeling a pang of loss for the raw bar and crab legs he loved so much. "Why?"

"Henry left," Wanda said. "Can't blame the guy after everything he's been through, and the owner decided it was more than he wanted to manage after all these years, so the building was put on the market just two days ago."

"It will probably sell fast," Drew said. Real estate was precious in Keating Hollow, and after all the growth they'd had in the past five to seven years, nothing stayed on the market long. That was true for both commercial and residential properties.

"Oh, it did," Wanda said with a gleam in her eye. "Do you remember that notorious show *Beachside with the Buchanans?*"

"That reality show?" Abby asked. "Don't they have like six spin-offs of that now?"

"Yep, that's the one. And yes, they keep doing more and more shows," Wanda said. "Their eldest appears to want to escape their fishbowl lifestyle, and he's moving here for some peace and quiet. I'm not sure what he wants to open at Woodlines, but it sounds like maybe another farm to table place."

"Their eldest?" Abby parroted. "You mean Anders Buchanan? The one who refused to be filmed for anything, *ever*, since he was like sixteen?"

"Yeah, he sued his parents to get out of it, I think," Wanda said. "Apparently he's looking for a quiet life away from it all, and Keating Hollow is it."

"Has anyone told him about the recent ghost possessions?" Noel joked. "I'm not sure quiet is how I'd describe Keating Hollow these days."

"Hey, don't jinx it," Drew said. "The law enforcement team is working very hard to ensure a safe and drama-free summer."

They all looked around at each other and then burst out laughing.

"Famous last words," Noel said and then raised her glass. "A toast to the birthday boy."

And then all together, every person Drew loved in the world raised their glasses and said, "To Drew. Happy Birthday."

DEANNA'S BOOK LIST

Witches of Keating Hollow:
Soul of the Witch
Heart of the Witch
Spirit of the Witch
Dreams of the Witch
Courage of the Witch
Love of the Witch
Power of the Witch
Essence of the Witch
Muse of the Witch
Vision of the Witch
Waking of the Witch
Honor of the Witch
Promise of the Witch
Return of the Witch

Fortune of the Witch
Song of the Witch

Keating Hollow Happily Ever Afters:
Gift of the Witch
Wisdom of the Witch
Light of the Witch

Witches of Befana Bay:
The Witch's Silver Lining
The Witch's Secret Love

Witches of Christmas Grove:
A Witch For Mr. Holiday
A Witch For Mr. Christmas
A Witch For Mr. Winter
A Witch For Mr. Mistletoe
A Witch For Mr. Frost
A Witch For Mr. Garland

Premonition Pointe Novels:
Witching For Grace
Witching For Hope
Witching For Joy
Witching For Clarity
Witching For Moxie
Witching For Kismet

Miss Matched Midlife Dating Agency:
Star-crossed Witch
Honor-bound Witch
Outmatched Witch
Moonstruck Witch
Rainmaker Witch

Jade Calhoun Novels:
Haunted on Bourbon Street
Witches of Bourbon Street
Demons of Bourbon Street
Angels of Bourbon Street
Shadows of Bourbon Street
Incubus of Bourbon Street
Bewitched on Bourbon Street
Hexed on Bourbon Street
Dragons of Bourbon Street

Pyper Rayne Novels:
Spirits, Stilettos, and a Silver Bustier
Spirits, Rock Stars, and a Midnight Chocolate Bar
Spirits, Beignets, and a Bayou Biker Gang
Spirits, Diamonds, and a Drive-thru Daiquiri Stand
Spirits, Spells, and Wedding Bells

Ida May Chronicles:
Witched To Death

DEANNA'S BOOK LIST

Witch, Please
Stop Your Witchin'

Crescent City Fae Novels:
Influential Magic
Irresistible Magic
Intoxicating Magic

Last Witch Standing:
Bewitched by Moonlight
Soulless at Sunset
Bloodlust By Midnight
Bitten At Daybreak

Witch Island Brides:
The Wolf's New Year Bride
The Vampire's Last Dance
The Warlock's Enchanted Kiss
The Shifter's First Bite

Destiny Novels:
Defining Destiny
Accepting Fate

Wolves of the Rising Sun:
Jace
Aiden

Luc
Craved
Silas
Darien
Wren

Black Bear Outlaws:
Cyrus
Chase
Cole

Bayou Springs Alien Mail Order Brides:
Zeke
Gunn
Echo

ABOUT THE AUTHOR

New York Times and USA Today bestselling author, Deanna Chase, is a native Californian, transplanted to the slower paced lifestyle of southeastern Louisiana. When she isn't writing, she is often goofing off with her husband in New Orleans or playing with her two shih tzu dogs. For more information and updates on newest releases visit her website at deannachase.com.

Made in the USA
Monee, IL
15 July 2025